Stephen W. Clark

Easy Lessons in Language

Stephen W. Clark

Easy Lessons in Language

ISBN/EAN: 9783337393045

Printed in Europe, USA, Canada, Australia, Japan

Cover: Foto ©Andreas Hilbeck / pixelio.de

More available books at **www.hansebooks.com**

IN THE NATIONAL SERIES.

EASY LESSONS

IN

LANGUAGE;

WITH

ILLUSTRATIONS AND DIAGRAMS.

By S. W. CLARK, A.M.

A. S. BARNES AND COMPANY,

NEW YORK AND CHICAGO.

1875.

Prof. S. W. Clark's Language Series.

GRADED COURSE.
{
1. EASY LESSONS IN LANGUAGE.
2. BRIEF ENGLISH GRAMMAR.
3. THE NORMAL GRAMMAR.
}

HELPS.
{
4. ANALYSIS OF THE ENGLISH LANGUAGE.
5. GRAMMATIC CHART.
6. KEY TO NORMAL GRAMMAR.
}

CONTENTS.

NOTE TO TEACHERS.

IN arranging the METHODS of instruction in this book, the Author puts himself in the position of the Teacher. Believing that with *young* pupils the most successful appeal is to their " common sense," he has so graded and stated the questions for class exercises that the little thinkers will generally find it more difficult to be wrong than right in their answers.

It is not intended to limit the teacher to the questions in the book ; these are given rather as samples of the author's methods of conducting oral exercises in Language Lessons. Many additional questions and illustrations will occur to the teacher as the various topics come up. *By all means and methods, let the little pupils triumph every time,* and thus gain courage for a new effort at the next recitation.

It is better to *wake up the minds* of children to independent thinking than to fill their memory with the words of others. Hence the plan of this book requires less of the discouraging drudgery of committing to memory, and more of judicious questions and lively oral teaching. But this METHOD makes necessary the closest attention of the pupils during class recitations.

One great duty of the teacher is to preserve, as far as possible, the natural simplicity—the unaffected eloquence of the child's speech.

It is only when that speech becomes vitiated by " evil communications " that "corrupt good manners," that the child's language, like his other habits, becomes corrupt.

Always connect your teaching of the Science with the practice of the Art. Let every day's exercise close with a permanent correction of some prominent error in Language.

PREFACE.

LANGUAGE is the first thing a child learns. The kindly expressions of a mother's face, the softened tones, the joyous smiles, speak the language of love to the heart of the child. And when WORDS have assumed their meaning to the little one, "A word fitly spoken is like apples of gold in pictures of silver."

The earliest stages of mental development are always accompanied by efforts to express thoughts and feelings. The wants of children demand less of any other branch of learning which our schools afford, than they do of language. Arithmetic and Geography can be postponed until commercial affairs may make them useful. But Language is indispensable to the every-day life of the little child, as really as to the man.

Language, then, ought to be the simplest of all studies; and it may be made so if we well adapt our methods of teaching it to the nature and capabilities of childhood.

This little book claims that adaptation. It has its outgrowth and its practical tests with children of younger years than usually study Grammar. In matter and in manner it is intended so to meet the wants and to gratify the tastes of children, as to make the study of Language, as also the practice of correct speech, an agreeable pastime.

This book does not claim to be a complete Grammar of our language. It has its place previous to Grammar, yet with just enough of the science and the art of Language to make every lesson a graded, preparatory step to the study of the author's " BRIEF ENGLISH GRAMMAR."

THE QUEEN OF

"GOOD ENGLISH"

TO HER YOUNG SUBJECTS,

Greeting:

MY DEAR LITTLE PEOPLE,—

In spite of all rivals, I am your queen, and have a right to preside at all your parties; and when you have decided what to say, to tell you how to say it. You must be loyal subjects of my government, using my words according to my laws.

2. In practice, many of you do "cherish, honor and obey" me. But you have not yet studied my laws. These you must learn. My servants will teach you some of the most important of them from this little book. I have caused them to be made plain, so that the smallest of you may understand them and learn how to obey them.

3. Of all the SCIENCES you will ever learn, the greatest is that of LANGUAGE; and the best language in the world is mine. The greatest of all ARTS is that of using WORDS.

4. Learn this art, and
    Your thinking will be more orderly and practical,
    Your speaking will be sensible and agreeable,
    Your progress in all school studies will be more rapid,
    Your delight in reading literary works will be greater,—
    You may yourselves become essayists and authors,—
    Your social position will be higher;—for thereby
    You will be better fitted for the society of cultivated people;
    You will learn how to write good sensible letters to your parents and friends.

5. Above all, do you desire to be useful? Pure, elegant language will give you the key to success in doing good. Accuracy in language favors uprightness of heart, and pure thoughts are all the better for being expressed in purest words.

6. Let me, then, as your loving queen, urge you to give diligent attention to the study of my laws.

7. Throughout all my provinces, you shall have good and competent teachers, who, with the aid of this little book, will teach you the laws of my empire, and set you good examples in obeying them.

8. But I would not have you satisfied with merely the SCIENCE of Language. Learn also the ART of rightly using words. In Language, as in all other arts, PRACTICE is most important. Without practice in the correct use of words, the definitions and theories of Grammar will be of little real benefit. Hence this book devotes much space to " PRACTICE" in Sentence-making, and to " CRITICISMS" of the more common errors of speech.

9. These exercises are only samples of what your skillful teacher will require and give in your daily recitations. *Covet criticism.* As you would thank your friend for brushing an obtrusive spider from your hair, or a coal mark from your clean face, so thank your teacher for every correction, private or public, she may make of any expression of your bad English.

10. By thus uniting correct practice with " sound doctrine "—care-fully observing the speech of our best writers and speakers—" imitating their virtues, and avoiding their errors "—you shall become masters of the Language, and honored subjects of your loving QUEEN OF GOOD ENGLISH.

*** Let each pupil read a paragraph of this speech, and then report to the class, in his own language, the substance of what he has read.

EASY LESSONS IN LANGUAGE.

LESSON I.

1. Children play.
   Who play ?

2. The boy runs. *Who* runs ?
   The boy *does* what ?

3. Little girls trundle hoops.
   What girls trundle hoops ?
   Little girls *do* what ?
   Little girls trundle *what ?*

4. Larger girls walk and talk.
   What girls walk and talk ?
   Larger girls *do what ?*

It has not been difficult for you to answer these questions correctly.

Does the picture answer those questions as you have ?

Do pictures speak ?   Do they give us thoughts ?

Then if we were artists, might we express many thoughts by pictures ?

But we are not all picture-makers.   How else may we express our thoughts ?

ALFRED. We may *speak* our thoughts.

MARY. We may *write* our thoughts.

CHARLES. If we have good thoughts, we may have them *printed* and preserve them forever.

Do we sometimes let people know what we think and how we feel by our *actions ?*   How do we know when ERNEST is *sad* and when he is *merry ?*

If your little brother should ask you where his ball is, could you tell him without saying a word ?   How ?

Now we have seen that there are many ways of giving and receiving thoughts—by *actions,* by *pictures,* by *words.*

LESSON II.

Language.

1. DEFINITION. *Any means of giving and receiving thoughts is called Language.*

Words.

In every-day life we study the language of actions and of pictures; their language is *natural* and requires not much study. But *word language* is artificial, and requires careful study to enable us properly to speak it and write it.

Words are signs. Signs of things and signs of thoughts.

When we talk about things we do not use the things themselves, but the *words* that are the *signs* of those things.

We cannot see a thought; but we can see the *sign* of it, the *word* that represents the thought.

We cannot hear a thought; but we can hear the *word spoken;* that is the sign of the thought.

Thoughts *came to us,* not from words alone, but from *things* which we may see, hear, smell, taste, and feel.

Our thoughts *go from us to others* through their *signs*— the words that represent them.

Words may be spoken and written.

CLASS may *write* on your slates five words each.

Now each may *speak* the words written.

Can we translate words made by the *voice* into words made by the *hand?*

I will *speak* five words, and you may catch them in the air, and place them on your slates: *Pen, pencil, slate, chalk, superintendent.* Write.

Can we translate *written* words into *sounds?*

I *write* on the blackboard four words, and you may *speak* them : *Nature, gymnastics, Cincinnati, Chicago, croquet.**

———◆———

LESSON III.

Names.

1. DEFINITION. *Words that stand for persons and things are Names.*

Everything has its name.   Every person has a name.
Each pupil may write his or her name on the slate.

PRACTICE.

MARY may write the names of three things we can *see.*
CORA may write the names of three things we can *hear.*
CLARA may write the names of three things we can *taste.*
ANNA may write the names of three things we can *smell.*
ERNEST may write the names of three things we can *feel.*
WILLIE may write the names of three things we cannot *see,* nor *hear,* nor *taste,* nor *smell,* nor *feel.*

Name Words—Nouns.

2. DEFINITION. People who write grammars say that " *all names are Nouns.* "

We may call them either *names* or *nouns ;* for they mean the same thing.

———

* NOTE TO TEACHERS.—In all exercises, let the spelling be carefully examined and the pronunciation be fully criticised.

PRACTICE.

As I read the following story, you may write it on your slates, and point out all the names found in it :*

"A little bird built a nest in the bushes in the back part of the garden. Julia found the nest. It had four speckled eggs in it. Julia did not disturb the nest, nor distress the little birds. One day she came home from a long visit, and ran into the garden to peep at the four tiny eggs. Instead of the four pretty eggs, there were only broken, empty shells. 'Oh,' she said, picking out the pieces, 'the beautiful eggs are broken and spoiled.' 'No, Julia,' said her brother, 'they are not spoiled. The best part of them have taken wings and flown away.'"

Now you may write every name, one over the other in columns, on your slates.

Who of you have found ten names in that story?

Who of you have found fourteen?

Who have found more?

I will now read the story again. Now write on your slates the answers to my questions.

What was the story about? Write.

What did the bird do? Where?

Who found the nest? What were in it?

What did Julia do to the nest? or not do?

After awhile what did Julia do?

---

* NOTE TO TEACHERS.—Whenever an exercise like this is given, it is well to require one of your pupils to write it, or a part of it, on the black-board for class criticism, each pupil, in turn, reporting orally any differences between the exercise on the black-board and that on his or her slate. Let the criticisms include the *spelling*, the proper *division into separate sentences*, the capital *letters*, the *punctuation marks*, and the marks for *quotations*. The teacher should always settle any differences by clearly stated decisions.

Did she find the eggs ?   Write.
What did she find ?   Write.
What did she say about it ?   Write.
What did her brother then say ?   Write.
What did he mean by "the best part of them ?"
Now can you put all these facts together, so as to make a complete story of it, and not have it all just like the story in the book ?   Try it and report to-morrow.

LESSON IV.

The Subject.

Class, what gives us light by day ?
ARTHUR. The *sun* gives us light by day.
William may place the sun on the blackboard.
WILLIAM. I cannot do that.   I can place the *name* of the sun there.
Then when we write or talk about a thing, do we use the *thing* itself or only the *name* of it ?
WILLIAM. We always use the *name.*
Donald may tell us what the sun *is.*
DONALD. The sun is a globe of light.
Connie may tell us three things that the sun *does.*
CONNIE. The sun *gives light.*
       The sun *gives heat.*
       The sun *shines.*

Remember—When we talk, we talk about something. And *that which we talk about is our Subject.*

What have we been talking about?
MARY. We have been talking about the *sun.*
Then what has been our *Subject ?*
Can we often say many things about one Subject ?

You may write on your slates these Sentences that I will give you, and tell me which is the Subject of each : *

3. *Birds* fly.
4. Fishes swim.
5. The sun shines.
6. The wind blows.
7. The snow melts.
8. The boy plays.
9. The boys play.
10. The *girl* sings.

11. The girls sing.
12. Can a parrot talk?
13. Will the dog bite?
14. The bird sings.
15. Some birds build nests.
16. Two boys fell into the river.

What Words.

2. *Remember—The Subject of a Sentence is always a Noun or some word or words used for a Noun.*

For Names—Pronoun.

3. *Remember—When any word is used "for a Noun," or instead of a Noun, it is called a Pronoun.*

The letter *I* is used *for the name* of any one who speaks, and is then a Pronoun.

The word *you* is used *for the name* of any one or more spoken to.

The words *he* and *she* are used *for the names* of some *persons* spoken of.

The word *it* is used *for the name* of some *thing* spoken of.

4. *Some Pronouns stand for many names.* Thus *we, ye, they* are used *for more names* than one.

---

* Let one pupil write them on the blackboard.

LESSON V.

The Predicate.

1. People talk.

> Of *whom* is something said here?
> Then what is the *Subject?*
> What do we *say* of "people?"

1. *Remember—The word that tells something of the Subject is called the Predicate.*

2. The sun *shines.*

> What word tells something of "the sun?"
> What then is the Predicate?

3. The wind blows.

> What is the *Predicate* of this Sentence?
> Why do you call "blows" the Predicate?

Because that word *tells* what the wind *does.*

PRACTICE.

You may write on your slates the Sentences I give you, and tell me which is the *Subject* and which word the *Predicate* of each.

4. The parrot talks.	9. The wind roars.
5. The owl screeches.	10. The dust flies.
6. The oriole sings.	11. The clouds collect.
7. The quail whistles.	12. The lightning flashes.
8. The hawk screams.	13. The thunder rolls.

Does it rain?

The Declaring Word—Verb.

2. *Remember—Every Predicate has in it at least one word that grammarians call a Verb.*

What is a verb?

3. DEFINITION. *A Verb is a word that declares something.*

John *studies.*

In this Sentence which word declares something?

Anna loves her doll.

What is the verb in this Sentence?
Why do you say "loves" is a Verb?

Other Words.

Remember—The Predicate often consists of other sorts of words united with the Verb.

John *studies.*—One word makes the complete Predicate.
John *is studying.*—Two words make the Predicate.
John *is studious.*—Two words make the Predicate.
John *is [a] student.*—"Is" and "student" make the Predicate.
John *has been studying.*—Three words make the Predicate.

We shall learn more about different sorts of words in Predicate in future Lessons. Meanwhile

Remember—In all Predicates *the last word* is the most important. For that tells *what is predicated* of the Subject. Other words in Predicate assist, (1) In making the statement; (2) In fixing the time; (3) In indicating the *manner* as actual or possible.

LESSON VI.

The Sentence.

1. *Remember—Every complete statement made by words is called a Sentence.*

2. All our speech is in Sentences.

3. *Every Sentence must have at least two parts. The Subject and the Predicate.*

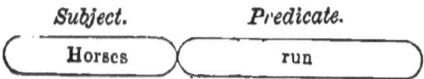

Is this a Sentence?   What is a Sentence?

4. DEFINITION. *A Sentence is such a group of words as declare something or ask a question.*

" People talk."   Why do you call this a Sentence?

Write—" Some very good people."

Is this a Sentence?

4. That is not a Sentence; for those words do not declare anything, nor ask a question.

PRACTICE.

I.

Read [or write] the following lines and say which are Sentences and which are not, and point out the Subject and the Predicate of each Sentence.

1. The Wren built her nest in the oyster-keg.
2. The nice little sparrow with striped head.
3. The Oriole is the most beautiful bird in the grove.
4. Those two Meadow Larks with speckled backs.

5. The night was cold, the Moon shone clear.
6. The large group of brilliant stars.
7. The comet with its fiery tail.
8. The world revolves on its axis.

II.

I write on the board the following Subjects. You may finish the Sentences by writing on **your** slates a suitable Predicate for each.

[Let each pupil report his Sentence.]

Now you may erase those Predicates and write others in their places—and report.

III.

I write on the board these five Predicates. You may fill the blanks with suitable Subjects.*

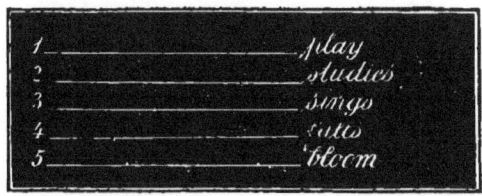

You may erase these Subjects and write other appropriate Subjects in the place of each. [Compare.]

---

* The Teacher will find extended *oral exercises* of this sort, lively and profitable.

LESSON VII.

The Object.

1. Birds fly.
2. Birds build nests.

"Birds fly."—Do they "fly" anything ?

"Birds build "———— Do they build anything ?

What do the birds build ?

DEFINITION. *The name of the person or thing that receives the action expressed by the Predicate, is called the Object.*

3. John saws ———— Saws *what?*
4. John saws *wood.*

You see that Sentence (3) is incomplete : for the verb "saws," expresses *such an action as requires an Object* to make the statement complete.

Remember 1. *Some verbs require Objects after them and some do not.*

Some that do—*Make, find, teach, pity, protect, &c.*
Some that do not—*Go, came, tarry, be, became, bloom.*

Remember 2. *The Object of a Sentence is always a Name or some word or words used for a Name.*

Remember 3. All these Pronouns may be Subjects of Sentences:

I study geography.—*who?* The *person* who is speaking.
You study grammar.—who? The *person* spoken to.
He recites well.—who ? The *boy* we speak of.
She recites better.—who ? The *girl* we speak of.
It is a good book.—what ? The *thing* we speak of.

Remember 4. Those Pronouns that may be Objects of Sentences are:

Me and *us* used *for names* of those who are speaking.

Thee and *you* used *for names* of persons spoken to.

Him, her, it, and *them,* used *for names* of persons spoken of.

We shall, in future lessons, find other Pronouns used as Objects.

PRACTICE.

I.

Write Sentences, using the Pronoun "me" as Object.
Write Sentences, using the Pronoun "us" as Object.
Write Sentences, using the Pronoun "you" as Object.
Write Sentences, using the Pronouns "him" and "her" as Objects.
Write Sentences, using the Pronoun "it" as Object.
Write Sentences, using the Pronoun "them" as Object.

LESSON VIII.

Sentences—Classes.

1. *Remember—Sentences that have no Objects are called Intransitive Sentences.*

EXAMPLES.

1. Julia weeps.	4. Flowers bloom.
2. Moses died.	5. Time flies.
3. Stars shine.	6. Trees grow.

2. *Remember—Sentences that have Objects are called Transitive Sentences.*

EXAMPLES.

1. Trees bear fruit.
2. William caught *rabbits.*
3. Dinah dresses *dolls.*

PRACTICE.

Fill the blanks with appropriate Subjects and Objects.

1. Now erase the *Subjects* and write new ones that will be appropriate.

2. Next erase the *Objects* and write others.

3. Try to supply Subjects and Objects that shall begin with the same letters as the Predicates.* Thus, *Cora corrected compositions. Samuel studies science.*

---

* To THE TEACHER.—The object of Lessons in Language should be to make our pupils *familiar with words* and *ready in the use of them.* Frequent practical exercises like the above, at the close of recitations, will be found interesting and profitable.

When we place a Transitive Sentence in diagram, we place the object to the right of the Predicate. Thus,

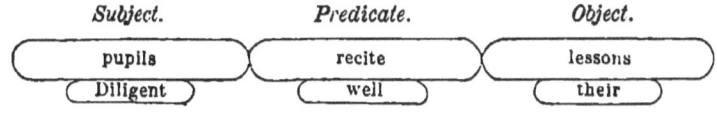

Subject.	*Predicate.*	*Object.*
pupils	recite	lessons
Diligent	well	their

PRACTICE.

Write on your slates the words that I speak. After you have written I will write on the board.

1. boys love fun.

Is your sentence written just like mine?

WILLIAM. I differ.

TEACHER. Wherein?

WILLIAM. I commence the Sentence with a CAPITAL LETTER B.

TEACHER. You are right. It is a law in Language that

Every separate Sentence should begin with a Capital Letter.

2. Boys love fun

TEACHER. Is this all right?

JAMES. It is not like mine. I have placed a period at the end of the Sentence, as we were taught in the Spelling Book.

Every separate Sentence should have a Period at its close.

II.

A boy sent this letter to his teacher as an apology for being absent from school. I copy it just as he wrote it:

" dear Miss smith i couldnt git to school Yesterday because i was out the Knight afore and hadnt no Lesson will you pleas Excuse me."

Each member of the class may copy and write on paper a criticism of this letter, and read it in to-morrow's exercise.

LESSON IX.

The following is Oliver's criticism of the letter given yesterday :

1. The letter is not dated. *"Every Letter should be dated."*

2. It commences with a small *d*. *"Every Sentence should begin with a Capital letter."*

3. The name of the teacher begins with a small letter. *"Every Name of a person should begin with a Capital letter."*

4. The small *"i"* should be a Capital. *"Every Pronoun 'I' should be a Capital letter."*

5. The words *couldn't, get, night, before, had not,* and *please* were improperly spelled.

6. The word *"no,"* should be *any.*

Adjuncts.

So far we have talked about only the *Principal Parts* of Sentences, the *Subject,* the *Predicate,* and the *Object.*

While these are all that are *necessary to form the framework* of a Sentence, other parts are often important as helps in expressing the true and entire thoughts in the statement. Thus,

"Boys swear,"

is a complete Sentence, making an unqualified statement. But it is hard on the boys to leave it thus ; so, for the relief of good boys, we may vary the statement by the use of the word "bad." The Sentence will then read,

"Bad boys swear."

Here this word "bad" limits the word "boys" so as to exclude from the statement all boys *not bad.* Again,

"Boys swear"—an unqualified statement.

"Good boys swear"—a qualified statement.

Both these are Sentences. But we hope the latter is not true. We may express the truth by taking away the word " good," or, what is better, by adding a *modifying word* to the Predicate. Thus,

<blockquote>" Good boys *never* swear."</blockquote>

Now we have a true, sensible statement concerning " good boys." And we see the importance of the word " never " in stating the truth.

1. DEFINITION. *A word used to limit or modify the meaning of another word is an Adjunct.*

  1. Girls study. | 2. *Little* girls study.

  3. *Three little* girls study.

  4. *Those three little* girls study *diligently.*

Here we say the same thing every time ; and every time we add something to the first statement "girls study."

Each word has its special use. Thus,

" Little " tells *what* girls—as to size.

"Three " tells *how many* girls.

"Those" tells *which* three little girls.

All these three words are joined to the word "girls," to describe "girls," telling *which, how many,* and *what kind.*

So also the word *"diligently"* is added to the word "study," telling *how* those three little girls study.

Classes.

We have only two sorts of Adjuncts :

1. Those that tell us *whose, what,* or *what kind* of things are mentioned. Such words are joined to *Nouns* and to *Pronouns,* and are called *Adjectives.*

2. Those that tell *how, why, when,* or *where* something is done. Such words are joined to *verbs,* sometimes to other words, and are called *Adverbs.*

So we may always tell what word is an Adjective—not by its *shape* but by its *use.* If it is *joined to a Noun* to modify its meaning, it must be an Adjective.

All other Adjuncts are Adverbs.

LESSON X.

Principal Elements.

1. *The Subject,* the *Predicate,* and the *Object* of a Sentence are called *Principal Elements.*

Offices.

The Principal Elements make the statement.

The Adjuncts vary or in some way modify the statement.

Let each pupil write a Sentence that has no Adjunct.

Let each pupil write a Sentence that has one Adjunct.

Let each pupil write a Sentence that has two Adjuncts.

2. In Diagrams we place an Adjunct beneath the word that it modifies. Thus,

In this Sentence " the " is an Adjunct of " sun." Hence we place it beneath " sun."

" Brightly " is an Adjunct of " shines." Hence its place in Diagram is beneath " shines."

PRACTICE.

I.

You may place a Diagram like this on the black-board (or on slates), and each pupil place one of these Sentences in it :

1. Large bodies move slowly. | No man works always.
2. Good boys study diligently. | Some men never work.
3. Some people act strangely. | Whence came those gypsies?

Now let each pupil write an original Sentence adapted to the same Diagram.

II.

" The summer days are coming,
  The blossoms deck the bough,
 The bees are gayly humming,
  And the birds are singing now."

How many lines in this exercise ?

How many Sentences ?—count them.

Does the first line make a complete Statement ?

What is the Subject ?

Why do you call "days" the Subject ?

What days are coming ?

What is the *Subject* of the second Sentence ?

What is *said* of "blossoms ?"   Then

What is the *Predicate* of that Sentence ?

Do the blossoms deck anything ?

What do they deck ?   Then

What word is the *Object?*

What is the Subject of the third Sentence ?

What is said of "the bees ?"

What is the Subject of the fourth Sentence ?

What are " the birds " doing ?

When are "the birds" singing?

Has this Sentence an Object stated ?

Why does each line commence with a Capital Letter ?

Because it is a law of language that

Every line in Poetry should begin with a Capital Letter.

Why does not every line end with a Period ?

Two or more Sentences, connected in sense as parts of the same general topic, require a Period only at the end of the last.

LESSON XI.

1. Each pupil **examine** this picture carefully, **and write on your** slate the name of everything you can see in it.

2. Now each may write complete Sentences :

(*a*) In the first Sentence, tell *what the horses are doing.*

(*b*) In the second Sentence, tell *what the dog is doing.*

(*c*) In the third Sentence, tell *what the birds are doing.*

(*d*) In the fourth Sentence, tell *what the children are doing.*

(*e*) In the fifth Sentence, tell *what the larger boy holds in his hand.*

(*f*) In the sixth, tell *what the little girl holds in her hand.*

(*g*) In the seventh, tell *what the larger boy seems about to do.*

(*h*) In the eighth, tell *what the other little boy seems about to do.*

(*i*) In the ninth, tell *what the little girl seems about to do.*

(*j*) In the tenth, tell *what you see on the ground between the children.*

(*k*) In the eleventh, tell *what you see behind the larger boy.*

3. Now tell what is the *Subject* of each Sentence ?

What is the *Predicate* of each Sentence ?

Which of the Sentences have an Object ?

Which of the Sentences have no Object ?

Review.

Sec p. 18. What is a *Sentence?*

" 22. What is an *Intransitive Sentence?*
Let each pupil make an Intransitive Sentence.

" 22. What is a *Transitive Sentence?*
Let each pupil make a Transitive Sentence.

" 18. *How many* Principal Parts *must* a Sentence have?

" 20. *How many* Principal Parts *may* a simple Sentence have?

" 14. What is the *Subject* of a Sentence?

" 15. *What sort* of words are used as Subjects of Sentences?
Let each pupil make an original Sentence having "*lion*" for the Subject.

" 16. What is the *Predicate* of a Sentence?

" 17. What sort of word must be in Predicate?
Let each pupil make a Sentence having the Verb "*makes*" as Predicate.

" 20. What is the *Object* of a Sentence?

" 21. What sort of words are used as Objects?
Let each pupil make a Sentence having the Noun "*house*" as its Object.

" 25. What is an *Adjunct?*
Let each pupil make a Sentence having the word *good* as Adjunct of the Subject.
Let each pupil make a Sentence having the word *green* as Adjunct of the Object.
Let each pupil make a Sentence having the word "*badly*" as Adjunct of the Predicate.

" 25. *What sort* of words must an Adjunct of Nouns and Pronouns be?

" 25. *What sort* of words are all other Adjuncts?

LESSON XII.

Analysis.

Little children seldom write long Sentences.

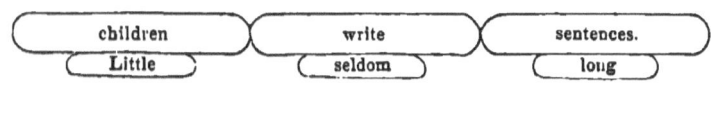

(A)

Of *whom* is something here said ?

Something is said of *children.*

What *is said* of children ?

Children *write.*

Children write *what?*

Children write *Sentences.*

What children write Sentences ?

Little children.

Little children write *what sort* of Sentences ?

Long Sentences.

When do little children write long Sentences ?

Seldom.

(B)

In this Sentence, for what do we use the word "little ?"

It is used to tell *what* children seldom write long Sentences.

What is the use of the word "children ?"

It is used to tell *who* seldom write long Sentences.

What is the use of the word "seldom?"

To tell *when* little children write long Sentences.

What is the use of the word " write ?"

It is used to tell what little children *do*.

What is the use of the word "long?"

It is used to tell *what* sort of Sentences children seldom write.

What is the use of the word "Sentences ?"

It is used to tell *what* little children write.

(c)

What is the *Subject* of this Sentence ?
Why do you call "children" the Subject ?
What *sort of word* is the word "children ?"
Why do you call that word a *Name?*
What is the *Predicate* of this Sentence ?
Why do you call " write " the Predicate ?
What *sort of word* is "write ?"
Why do you call it a *Verb?*
What is the *Object* of this Sentence?
Why do you call " Sentences " the Object ?
What *sort of word* is " Sentences ?"
Why do you call "Sentences " a *Noun?*
What are the *Adjuncts* of this Sentence ?
Why do you call "little" an Adjunct of "children ?"
Why do you call "seldom" an Adjunct of "write ?"
Why do you call "long" an Adjunct of Sentences ?

NOTE. The teacher will select other Sentences for Analyses, as may seem appropriate.

LESSON XIII.

Combined Sentences.

1. Robins built nests in our garden.
2. Orioles built nests in our garden.
3. Wrens built nests in our garden.
4. Sparrows built nests in our garden.
5. Blue-Jays built nests in our garden.

Here are five Single Sentences, all having the same words except the Subjects.

Can we express the same facts in fewer words?

6. Robins and Orioles and Wrens and Sparrows and Blue-Jays built nests in our garden.

This Sentence includes all the others. It is one Sentence made up of parts of other Sentences. We call such Sentences *Compound Sentences.*

What is a Compound Sentence?

DEFINITION. *A Compound Sentence is a Sentence made by uniting parts of two or more Single Sentences.*

7. Ducks lay eggs. ⎫
8. Hens lay eggs. ⎬ Ducks, hens and birds lay eggs.
9. Birds lay eggs. ⎭

Notice that in the above Compound Sentence the word *and* is placed between the words having the same construction. When there are more than two words thus united in a Compound Sentence we usually omit all the conjunctions but the last, and put commas in their places. Thus,

Robins, Orioles, Wrens, Sparrows and Blue-Jays.

PRACTICE.

I.

Write these *Single Sentences* on your slates and combine them into *Compound.*

(a) 1. Wind blows the dust.
       2. Wind purifies the air.
       3. Wind drives the ships.

(b) 4. Wind propels the ships.
       5. Steam propels the ships.

(c) 6. Mr. Smith sells hats.
       7. Mr. Smith sells caps.
       8. Mr. Smith sells robes.

(d) 9. Sheep feed upon the mountains.
     10. Goats feed upon the mountains.
     11. Cows feed upon the mountains.

II.

Resolve these Compound Sentences into the equivalent Single Sentences.

1. " The massy fountains and the sylvan shades,
    The dreams of Pindus and the Aonian maids,
    Delight us no more."

2. " The tender lambs He raises in His arms
    Feeds from his hands and in his bosom warms."

3. Willie rides a nice, little, black, three-year-old, Shetland pony.

III.

4. Each pupil make a Sentence having two Subjects.

5. Each pupil make a Sentence having two Predicates.

6. Each pupil make a Sentence having two Objects.

7. Each pupil make a Sentence having three Subjects.

8. Each pupil make a Sentence having three Predicates.

LESSON XIV.

Connectives.

Three *and* four are seven.

"*And* means *add*."

Anna went to the lecture.

Lucy went to the lecture.

Because each Sentence has the same Predicate we may unite the Subjects and make one Predicate common to both. Thus,

Anna and Lucy went to the lecture.

You see the word "and" is used only to join together "Anna" and "Lucy" as Subjects of the same Predicate.

"*Conjoin* means *join together*." Hence,

DEFINITION. *A word that joins together other words is called a Conjunction*.

Conjunctions may join together two or more.

Subjects. *Cora* and *Eddie* sing sweetly.

Predicates. Mary *sings* and *plays* and *studies.*

Objects. Ernest studies *Geography* and *Grammar.*

Adjectives. A *great* and *good* man has gone.

Adverbs. *Slowly* and *sadly* they climb the mountain.

The conjunctions in most common use are *and, but, or, nor.*

These and some others join words that have *similar uses.*

Another class of conjunctions join *words* to *sentences.*

I will go with you *if you call.*

Here "if you call" makes "will go" conditional. "If" connects the conditional Sentence to "will go."

I went *because he invited me.*

" Because he invited me " tells *why* " I went."

" Because " introduces the Adverbial Sentence and connects it to the verb " went." It is therefore a Conjunction.

I will go *when John returns.*

"When John returns " is an Adverbial Sentence, because it tells *when* " I will go."

" When " introduces the Adverbial Sentence, and connects it to " will go." It is therefore a Conjunction.

DEFINITION. *All words that join Adverbial Sentences to the verbs which they modify are Adverbial Conjunctions.*

Adverbial Conjunctions in most frequent use are *if, though, unless, since, for, because, where, when, after, before, while.*

1. William has not been here *since you left.*
2. " *Where thou lodgest,* I will lodge."
3. I reached the station *after the cars had left.*
4. " *When the cock crew,* he wept."
5. " *Before the cock crow,* thou shalt deny me thrice."
6. " Look *before you leap.*"
7. " If sinners entice thee, consent thou not."

PRACTICE.

1. Make a Sentence that shall have " and " join two Nouns.
2. Make a Sentence that shall contain " or."
3. Make a Sentence that shall contain two Conjunctions.
4. Write a Sentence making " and " connect two Subjects.
5. Write a Sentence making " or " connect two Subjects.
6. Write a Sentence making " or " connect two Predicates.
7. Write a Sentence making " or " connect two Adjuncts.

LESSON XV.

Exclamations.

" Hark ! the pealing,
Softly stealing,
Evening bell ;
Sweetly echoes
Down the dell."

Remember—A word used only to denote some surprise or any sudden or intense feeling, is called an Exclamation.

What Exclamatory word in the lines above ?

Exclamations usually have this mark (!) placed after them.

Remember—When the last part of two or more words have similar sounds they are said to be *rhyming words*.

What rhyming words are in the above lines ?

Which line does not rhyme with the other ?

Remember—When we borrow words or Sentences from some other author we place " double commas " before and after the borrowed words. These we call *Quotation marks*.

Do you see any double commas on this page ?

Interrogations.

" Oh, why does the white man follow my path,
Like the hound on the tiger's track ?
Does the flush on my dark cheek waken his wrath ?
Does he covet the bow at my back ?

Does that Sentence *declare* something or *ask* something ?

Remember—When we write or print *questions,* we place a mark like this (?) after them.

Do you see a *question mark* at the end of the second line ?

What sort of Sentences always require such marks ?

Do you see any other question marks in the stanza ?

Do you know what is the difference between an *Interrogative Sentence* and a *Declarative Sentence ?*

" Does he covet the bow at my back ? "

He does covet the bow at my back.

Here are the same words in each Sentence.

Are both Sentences alike ?　How can we change *Asking Sentences* into *Declaring Sentences ?*

Do you see an *Exclamation* in the first line?

Do those lines end in rhyming words ?

Are all these Sentences *Transitive?*

Why are *Double Commas* placed at the beginning of the Stanza ?　Should there not be one at the end of the last line ?

Change these Asking Sentences to Declaring Sentences :

    1. " Did you see the comet? "
    2. " Can love be bought with gold ?"
    3. Should every pupil learn to make Sentences?
    4. Will you go to the lecture to-night?

Change these Declaring Sentences to Asking Sentences.

    1. The printing press is a blessing to the world.
    2. The telegraph is a modern invention.
    3. Swift's comet was discovered this year.
    4. The moon is over two hundred thousand miles from us.
    5. Every man is master of his own fortune.

MODEL. Is the printing press a blessing to the world ?

"THE CHILDREN AT HOME."

ERNEST. Sister Anna, did Miss Lester say, that in all our talking, we use only nine different words?

ANNA. No, Ernest, not nine different *words*, but nine different *sorts* of words.

ERNEST. What! only nine sorts of words in all we say? and all Miss Lester says too?

ANNA. Yes, that is all any body uses; for she said to our class in "Easy Lessons in Language," that all the books we read—all the sermons and speeches we hear—are made of only nine sorts of words, and that the great DICTIONARY contains only so many sorts.

ERNEST. Does she mean that the *shortest* words are one sort, and the words of *two* syllables are another sort, and so on to nine?

ANNA. O, no; the "different sorts" mean different *uses* in making Sentences; and there are only nine different things that words do.

ERNEST. What are they?

ANNA The most important thing that words do is to give *names* to every thing: for she says "every thing has a name; and all names are *Nouns*." That is one sort. But a few words are used instead of Nouns. These she calls *Pronouns*, which means *for* Nouns.

ERNEST. Is that another sort?

ANNA. That is *called* another sort, but the Pronouns really have the same uses as the Nouns, only it is a little more elegant to use them once in a while, than to use the Nouns every time.

ERNEST. What next?

ANNA. Another sort always go with Nouns and Pronouns to *describe* things—telling *which* things, *whose*, or *what kind* of things are mentioned. These she calls *Adjectives*.

ERNEST. That makes three sorts—Nouns, Pronouns and Adjectives.

ANNA. The next sort are called *Verbs*, because they are the *speaking words*,—they *tell* what folks *do* and what things *are*.

And another sort generally go with Verbs to tell *when*, *where*, or *how* things are done. Miss Lester calls these *Adverbs*, because they are *added* to Verbs. These five sorts are all we need in making Sentences.

ERNEST. Then why not say we have but *five* sorts of words?

ANNA. Because we have a few words used for other purposes. One sort join other words together,—just as the sign "plus" in Arithmetic joins numbers together. These are called *Conjunctions*, because they join. Then we have *Prepositions*—so called because they are *placed before* other parts of Phrases. I do not know exactly what that means; for we have not studied that subject yet, but it *is so*, "because the teacher says it is."

ERNEST. That does not make it so. Teachers sometimes make mistakes, just like other folks. What next?

ANNA. Words of the eighth sort are called *Exclamations*, because we exclaim with them when we get excited about something.

Then there are those words we use only to make our speech sound a little more pleasant. She calls these "Euphonics," or words of *Euphony*. That makes nine sorts, and that is all.

ERNEST. Does Miss Lester really mean to say that all the words in this UNABRIDGED DICTIONARY belong to one of those sorts of words?

ANNA. Yes. And if you should cut out every word there—one at a time—I can place them all in the nine ballot-boxes in papa's office, and have only one sort in a box.

ERNEST. I would like to see it done, for then we could put labels on the boxes, and know just where to find the words we want when we write compositions.

LESSON XVI.

Names—Nouns—Classes.

Every thing has its name. Some names belong in common to whole classes of persons and things, some to individual persons.

Thus, when we were very young we all had the same name—we were called *infants*. After that we were called *children*. These names were *common* to all of us. But at some time our parents gave to each one of us a special name, to distinguish us from other children—one perhaps being called Henry, another Robert, another Clara, and another Anna, so that each one has a *special* name—a *Proper* name. Hence, we say,

Names are of two sorts, $\left\{\begin{array}{l} \textit{Common names} \text{ and} \\ \textit{Proper names.} \end{array}\right.$

Common.

What is a Common Noun ?

A Common Noun is the name of classes or sorts of persons or of things.

Child, boy, girl, man, city, state are Common Nouns.

Proper.

What is a Proper Noun ?

A Proper Noun is the name of an individual person or place.

Ernest, Cora, John, Chicago, Iowa, Ganges are Proper Nouns.

This distinction of names is of practical use only when we write or print them. Thus, it is customary to write and print *common names* with the ordinary letters. But—

Every Proper Noun should begin with a Capital Letter.

PRACTICE.

1. Write on your slates these lines as I read them :

    1. If England were my place of birth,
    2. I'd love her tranquil shore ;
    3. Or if Columbia were my home,
    4. Her freedom I'd adore ;
    5. Tho' pleasant days in both I've pass'd,
    6. I dream of days to come ;
    7. O steer my bark to Erin's isle,
    8. For Erin is my home.

2. Now draw a line under each Noun.

3. Draw a second line under each Proper Noun.

Have you begun each line with a Capital Letter ?

Where do you place commas ?

Where have you placed semicolons?

Remember—When we wish to omit one or more letters in a written or printed word, we place a comma over the space made by the omission.

In the 2d line of the above stanza what letters are omitted between "I" and "d"? In the 4th line ?

In the 5th line after "Tho"? Between "I and "ve"?

In the 7th line have you placed a comma over "Erin's"?

Modifications—Number.

    Boy,   Girl—how many ?
    Boys,   Girls—how many ?

Every name commonly stands for *one* person or thing.

When we wish it to include *more than one* we change its *form.* Thus,

If I say *pen*, you know I mean *but one.*

If I say *pens*, you know I mean *more than one.* But you do not know the exact number. That must be determined by the use of some other word—as, *two* pens, *ten* pens. So we have only two forms of Names to denote *number.*

LESSON XVII.

Singular.

The common form which means but one we call Singular Number.

Plural.

The other form that means any number more than one we call the Plural Number.

Of what Number are the words *book, girl, doll, house, pencil?*

Of what Number are the words *books, girls, dolls, houses, pencils?*

If I say " there are ten *boy* in this room," am I giving the right form to all my words ? If I say " one *girls*," am I speaking correctly ?

Have we learned how we make a Name mean more than one ?

ROBERT says " we add *s* to the Noun to make it mean more than one. But if we mean ten, we say "ten" and also add s.

That is true so far as we have seen yet—

Because *nearly all our Nouns form their Plurals by the addition of s.* This is called the *Regular way* of forming Plurals.

PRACTICE.

Write the Plural forms of these words—

Sun.	Cloud.	River.
Moon.	Vapor.	Lake.
Star.	Mist.	Bay.
World.	Meteor.	Ocean.

You may now write on your slates the Singular forms of these words :

Horses.	Trees.	Vines.
Mules.	Plants.	Canes.
Carts.	Flowers.	Shrubs.

Irregular.

But some words do not form their Plurals by adding s.

Man means one.
Men means more than one.

Ox means one.
Oxen means more than one.

This is called the *Irregular method* of forming Plurals.

Here are a few of the most common Irregular words :

Child,	children.	Goose,	geese,	Staff,	staves.
Man,	men.	Mouse,	mice.	Shelf,	shelves.
Woman,	women.	Tooth,	teeth.	Wife,	wives.
Foot,	feet.	Ox,	oxen.	Life,	lives.

PRACTICE.

Change the Subjects to their Plural forms and the other parts of the Sentences to correspond.

1. The child of my uncle is my cousin.
2. The chief man of the common council was called Alderman.
3. The woman who lectures to-night is an eloquent lady.
4. A mouse was caught by our cat.
5. The goose is said to have saved Rome by screaming.
6. The foot of a duck is webbed.
7. A false tooth is not always an ornament.
8. The ox knoweth his owner.

MODEL—The children of my uncle are my cousins.

Change the Subjects of these Sentences to their Singular form and change the other words to correspond.

1. " The mists of the morning are rolling away."
2. The boys have had a lively time at recess.
3. The little girls delight to play croquet.
4. " The waves mount up and wash the face of heaven."

MODEL—The mist of the morning is rolling away.

LESSON XVIII.

The "Persons" of Nouns.

Remember—When a Noun is used to explain who is meant by the words "I" and "me," it is said to be of the First Person.

"I *John* saw these things."

"Pity me a poor *slave* to appetite."

Here "John" is the Proper name of the person who was speaking, and explains who was meant by "I." And "slave" is the Common name of the person who was speaking, and explains who was meant by "me."

Remember—When a Noun is the Name of a person spoken to, it is said to be of the Second Person.

"Ye *crags* and *peaks!* I am with *you* once again."

"*John,* have *you* seen my new kite?"

Here "crags," "peaks," and "John" are names of the person or things spoken to.

Remember—All names of persons and of things spoken of, are of the Third Person.

"There is a beautiful *world,*
Where *saints* and *angels* sing:
A *world* where *peace* and *pleasure* reign,
And heavenly *praises* ring."

Which Nouns in those four lines are spoken of?

Remember—Every Noun is of the *Third Person* except when it is used to explain who is meant by the Pronouns *I, me, we,* or *us*—of the First Person; and, *thou, thee, you,* or *ye*—of the Second Person.

When Nouns and Pronouns of the Third Person are used as Subjects of Sentences, we add *s* to the first Verb in Predicate when it denotes Present time.

I (Robert) love to sing..............*First*, or speaking person.
You, Sarah, love to sing...........Second, or spoken to.
The other Sarah love*s* to sing.......Third, or spoken of.

In the last Sentence *s* is added to the Verb "love" because "the other Sarah" is spoken of.

CRITICISM. Is it correct to say, My grandmother who *live* at our house *give* me some new present every time I gets one at school.

Correct the errors in that Sentence, and also in the following :

1. *Do* Aunt Fanny visit you often ?
2. *Has* you seen my new doll?
3. Anna *say* it *look* beautiful.
4. The little girl love to sing, and she sing very well.

The Cases of Nouns.

Case in Grammar means *condition*.

1. If a Noun or a Pronoun is *Subject* of a Sentence, it is in the *Subjective Case.*

"Mary had a little lamb."—"Mary" is in the Subjective Case.
"It followed her to school one day."—"It" is in the Subjective Case.

2. If a Noun or a Pronoun is the *Object* of a Sentence or of a Phrase, it is in the *Objective Case.*

"Mary had a little lamb."—"Lamb" is in the Objective Case.
"It followed her to school one day."—"Her" and "school" are in the Objective Case.

3. Nouns do not vary in form to denote their Case.

4. Pronouns (except *you, it, that, which,* and *what*) have different forms to denote their Case. [See p. 51.]

LESSON XIX.

Pronouns.

" Mary has a little lamb."
She pets it.

Who pets it?

Mary.

Then " she " means " Mary."
Does it *always* mean Mary?

She feeds *it*.

She feeds *what?*

Lamb.

Then " it " means " lamb."
Does it always?

" It followed *her* to school one day."
It followed *whom?*

Mary.

Then " her " means " Mary " this time.

We know that every thing has a Name, and when we make a statement about a person or thing, we generally use the name ; but we have a few little words that will sometimes answer just as well as the name, and better. Thus,

Ernest has a new book. Ernest's new book has beautiful pictures in Ernest's new book. Ernest's new book has nice stories. Ernest's new book has a red cover. The red cover has gold letters on the red cover.

When I read this story to Ernest's little sister, whose teacher thinks she is " too young to study Grammar," she said : " Papa, that story is true enough, but I think it is awkwardly told. If I were to write it, I would say—

" Ernest has a new book. *It* has beautiful pictures in *it*. *It* has nice stories. *It* has a red cover, *which* has gold letters on *it*."

Wherein do these forms differ ? and which is the better?

Pronouns—Personal.

A Pronoun is a word used instead of a Noun.

We have only about twenty words that are always used as Pronouns. Hence the same little Pronouns may stand for more than a thousand different Nouns at different times.

Remember—Fifteen of the Pronouns are called Personal Pronouns.

Not because they always stand for the names of *persons*, but because each one *is restricted in its use* to represent one of the three following classes of Nouns. Thus,

1. *I* and *me, we* and *us* always stand for names of persons *speaking*.

These are therefore of the *First Class*, called *First Person*.

2. *Thou* and *thee, ye* and *you* always stand for the names of persons *spoken to*.

These are of the *Second Class*, called *Second Person*.

3. *He* and *him, she* and *her, it, they,* and *them* always stand for the names of persons and things *spoken of*.

These are of the *Third Class*, called *Third Person.**

CAUTION.—In using Pronouns in Sentences we should select the right words. Thus,

(1.) We may use *I, we, thou, he, she, ye,* and *they* as Subjects of Sentences.

(2.) *Me, us, thee, him, her* and *them* may be used as Objects. These may also be used as Objects of Phrases.

(3.) *You* and *it* may be used as Subjects and Objects.

---

* Grammarians have a curious custom of applying the term "person" to *things* as well as to *people*. So that when they say "Third Person," they mean that the *man*, or *animal*, or *thing* is spoken *of*.

LESSON XX.

In the following Sentences, (1) Which are the Personal Pronouns ? (2) For what name is each Pronoun used ? (3) Is it of the *First*, of the *Second*, or of the *Third* Person.

1. " I came not here to talk."
2. " You know too well the story of our thraldom."
3. " We are slaves."
4. " Thou art perched aloft on the beetling crag."
5. " Ye crags and peaks! I am with you once again."
6. " He brought me to the banqueting house."
7. " She hath done what she could "
8. " They are all gone from the mountain house."
9. " Them that honor me, I will honor."
10. " It was sad to see her lift him from the gutter."

What is the *Subject* of each Sentence ?

What is the *Predicate* of each Sentence ?

Let each pupil make Sentences, using one of the Subject Pronouns in the first class.

Each pupil make Sentences, using as Object one of the Pronouns in the second class.

Each pupil make a Sentence for each of the Pronouns in the third class as Subject—and then, in other Sentences, use them as Objects.

MODELS—1. Are *you* fond of skating? *It* is pleasant exercise.

2. Practice *it* moderately and it will benefit *you*.

THE OLD SAMPLER.*

It was Thanksgiving evening: and half a dozen boys and girls who were gathered about their Quaker grandmother, whom they loved very dearly, urged her to tell them a story. " What will ye

---

* We requested a little girl, ten years old, to write an original story that should contain *all the Pronouns.* The above is Anna's story. We give it to the printer in her own manuscript, just as she wrote it.

have?" she asked, smilingly. "Oh, tell us about that old sampler that is hanging up in the chimney corner," they all cried, so she began. "When I was a little girl it was the fashion to work samplers, and my four sisters and I were almost crazy to work some, but as we had no patterns; all that could be done was to wish and wait. But one day our father went on his semi yearly visit to town, and stayed a week or more." Just then one of the children broke out "Then was when you got your first letter wasn't it grandma?" "I believe thou knowest as much about it as I do Robert?" said she, "and I guess I will not tell thee the rest." "Oh we dont know it grandma if Robbie does," said the others; so she resumed "Two or three days after he went away, my brother brought a letter from him from the post office, directed to me but it really was to all of us. He said that he had bought five different sampler patterns, which were very pretty, and he would bring them with him on his return. In about a week he came, bringing the patterns, which we all admired, and I chose the one with the border of ears of wheat, and worked a little semi circle of them in the corner, in which I worked my name and age. Does thee see it?"

Class will criticise the story on the following points—

1. Does it contain all the Personal Pronouns ?

2. Are the Capital Letters properly placed ?

3. Are the Periods all properly inserted ?

4. Some of the Commas and Semicolons are improperly placed ; will you correct the mistakes ?

5. Are the Quotation marks properly placed ?

6. Is the language all good English ?

Each of you please write an original story that shall contain all the Personal Pronouns, and bring it to recitation to-morrow.

LESSON XXI.

Relative Pronouns.

1. In addition to the list of Pronouns given in the last Lesson, we have other words used for Nouns.

Five of them always perform a *double office* in the Sentence.

1. They stand for *Nouns*.

2. They introduce *Adjective Sentences*, and connect them to the Nouns which those Sentences describe.

The boy *who* owns this book may rise.

What boy may rise ?   The boy *who owns this book*.

Then "who owns this book" is a Sentence, used here to describe "boy," telling *which* boy ; and the word "who" stands for "boy," and connects its sentence to "boy."

LIST.

Who, which, what, and *that* may be used as Subjects.

Whom, which, what, and *that* may be used as Objects.

The boy *who* has the knife *which* I lost.

What boy ?   Which knife ?

These five Pronouns are called by most grammarians *Relative Pronouns*. They are also called *Conjunctive Pronouns,* because they *join Sentences* to *Nouns.**

---

* Teachers and pupils will notice that the chief distinction between *Conjunctions* and *Conjunctive Pronouns* is that a word that is simply a Conjunction connects *similar elements—i. e.,* Nouns to Nouns, Verbs to Verbs, Adjectives to Adjectives, and Adverbs to Adverbs. Whereas Conjunctive Pronouns always connect an *Adjective Sentence* to a *Noun* or to a *Pronoun* for which this Pronoun stands.

CAUTION. In the use of Conjunctive Pronouns, be careful to use the right words. Thus,

Who and *whom* should stand for the names of *persons* only.

Which and *what* should stand for the names of *places* and *things.*

That may stand for the names of *persons* and of *things.*

The boy *who* studies. The boy *whom* I saw.

The book *which* I lost. She hath done *what* she could.

Those *boys that* have good lessons shall have the rewards *that* I promised.

Is it proper to say, The boy who I saw?

Is it correct to say, The boy *who* I gave the book to?

Interrogative.

When these four are used in asking questions, they are called *Interrogative Pronouns*. When thus used they do not *connect their Sentences* to Nouns.

Who has my knife?   *Whom* did you see?
What do you want?   *Which* will you have?

PRACTICE.

Point out the Pronouns in the following sentences, and tell their class.

1. " Them that honor me I will honor."
2. " Who will show us any good?"
3. " Some deemed him wondrous wise."
4. " She points them to the pure shrine which crowns the summit of the hill of science."
5. " What can compensate for loss of character?"
6. " Ye crags and peaks! I am with you once again."

CAUTION. Do not use " who " as the object of a Sentence, nor of a Phrase.

Wrong. Who did William marry?
   Say, *whom* did William marry?
Wrong. Who did you give the book to?
   Say, to *whom* did you give the book?
Wrong. I know not *whom* else were invited.
   Say, I know not *who* else were invited.

LESSON XXII.

Adjective Pronouns.

Besides the Pronouns that are *always* used instead of Nouns, we have a large class of other words that may be thus used whenever we need them. They are commonly used as *Adjectives*. Thus,

Good people are respected.

What is the *Subject* of this Sentence ?

What *Adjunct* of the Subject ?

Why do you call " good " an *Adjective* ? [See p. 66.]

The *good* are respected.

What is the Subject of this Sentence ?

Is the word "good " a Noun ?

"Good " is not a name, and therefore is not a Noun.

For what is the word "good " used ?

It is used *instead of the Noun* "people," and it also tells *what sort* of people.

Because it tells *what sort* of people, " good " is an *Adjective ;* and because it is *used instead of* " people," "good " is a *Pronoun.*

Grammarians call such words *Adjective Pronouns.*

When does an Adjective become an *Adjective Pronoun?*

DEFINITION. *An Adjective becomes an Adjective Pronoun whenever it is used instead of the Noun it modifies.*

The *rich* —— pity the *poor* ——.
The *wise* instruct the *ignorant.*

OBSERVE we place the word " the " before an Adjective when we make it an Adjective Pronoun.

PRACTICE.

What Adjective Pronouns are in these Sentences ?
1. " The vain, the wealthy, and the proud in folly's maze advance."
2. " The patient in spirit is better than the proud in spirit."
3. " The blind receive their sight, and the lame walk."
4. " The *ransomed* of the Lord shall return."
5. " The redeemed shall walk there."

Make a Sentence that has the Adjective Pronoun " bad " as Subject.
Make a Sentence that has the word "joyous" as Subject.
Make a Sentence that has the word "small" as Object.

[The teacher will require other exercises of this sort until the use of Adjectives as Adjective Pronouns shall become familiar to her pupils.]

CAUTION 1. Never use the Pronouns *I, we, thou, he, she* or *they* as the Object of a Sentence or of a Phrase.
Are the Pronouns in these Sentences properly used ?
1. Only they that call on us will we visit.
2. Will you permit Anna and I to go to the concert?
3. The teacher politely invited Seth and I to remain after school.
4. They that honor me I will honor.

2. Never use the Pronouns *me, thee, him, her, us,* or *them* as the Subject of a Sentence.

Are these Sentences correct ?

1. Mother, may *us girls* have a little dance in the parlor ?
2. John and me went to the same school.
3. Jane was there too ; her and me rode in the first boat.
4. Has thee been to the yearly meeting?

3. Never use the Pronouns *they* nor *them* for a Noun of the Single Number.
1. Let any boy guess this riddle if *they* can ?
2. Gold or silver will be paid if *they* are demanded.
3. No boy had as much applause as *they* deserved.
4. If any boy has my knife I will thank them to return it.
[Correct all the errors and report.]

LESSON XXIII.

Verbs.

1. *Verbs* declare acts or events.

2. Verbs are used—

    1. *In Sentences as Predicates.* I *love.*

    2. *In Phrases as Subsequents.* To *study.*

        1. I recite—Is this a Sentence ?

        2. I recited—Is this a Sentence ?

Do both these Sentences declare the *same act?*

Why should there be a difference in their forms?

        I recite when ?

        I recited when ?

Then the difference in form is made to show a difference in the *time* of the act.

        3. I recite—Is this a Sentence.

        4. You recite—Is this a Sentence ?

        5. John recites—Is this a Sentence?

Do all these Sentences state the same act ? Yes.

Do all denote the *same time* of the act ?   Yes.

Why then should there be a difference in their *forms?*

Please prepare to tell us to-morrow. [Consult p. 45.]

Changes.

3. *Verbs in Predicate have two changes of form.*

1st. To agree with their Subjects in Person and *Number.*

2d. To denote *past time.*

Present Form.

4. *The common form of a Verb denotes Present Time.*

I recite.   You love.   John walks.

Past Form.

5. *But if we wish to declare the act as past, we add "d" or "ed" to the Verb.*

I recited.   You loved.   John walked.

This method of changing the form of Verbs to denote past time is called the *Regular Method*—since most Verbs are thus changed.

Irregular.

6. But some Verbs are changed in form differently, and are therefore called *Irregular Verbs.* The most common of these are—

Present form.. Be, do, · go,   feel, lie, teach, know, see.
Past form ... Was, did, went, felt, lay, taught, knew, saw.

PRACTICE.

Fill the blanks in the following Sentences with appropriate Verbs.

1. I —— to school every day.
2. Sarah —— her lesson very well.
3. Children —— always fond of music.
4. John may —— after school to —— his lesson.

Let each member of the class write a Sentence having the verb "study" as Predicate, and the act as done yesterday.

Let each pupil use the verb "go" as declaring an act that John performed last week.

Let each pupil use the verb "see," and let the story be about something that took place this morning.

LESSON XXIV.

Future Form.

2. If we wish to represent a *future act,* we use *two verbs* in Predicate, one to *declare the act,* called the *Principal Verb,* and the other to denote the *time as future,* called an *Auxiliary Verb.*

I *shall recite.*   You *will love.*   John *will walk.*

In these Sentences " recite," " love," and " walk " are the Principal Verbs. "Shall" and " will " are *Auxiliary or helping verbs,* because they are used to help fix the time.

3. After the Pronouns *I* and *we* the Auxiliary Verb *shall* is used. At all other times *will* is used to denote a future act.

I *shall go* to-morrow.   You *will go* to-morrow.

An *Auxiliary Verb* is a little verb used in Predicate with another verb, or with a Participle, to denote the *time* or the mode of the action expressed by the Principal Verb.

The Auxiliary Verbs used *only with other verbs* are—

May,   can,   shall,   will,
Might,   could,   should,   would.

The Auxiliary Verbs used *only with Participles, Adjectives,* or *Nouns* are—

Am or *be,   has,   have,*
Was,   had.

PRACTICE.

Fill the blanks with appropriate Auxiliary Verbs.

1. I —— not go to the fair to-morrow.
2. —— you go to the lecture this evening?
3. I think John —— not attend.
4. Each pupil write a short story, telling what you think of doing to-morrow.

5. Each pupil write a story, telling what three things it may be well to do on next Christmas.

Let the following Sentences be so changed as to make the time *present*.

1. "The secretary stood alone."
2. "The king shall have my service."
3. The hero hath departed.
4. Like a spirit it came, in the van of a storm.
5. Sweet was the sound, when oft at evening's close.
6. Up yonder hill the village murmur rose.
7. I saw an eagle, wheeling near its brow.

MODEL. The secretary *stands* alone.

Let the following Sentences be so changed as to make it proper to add the word "*yesterday*" after each verb.

1. "The dishes of luxury *cover* his table."
2. "The voice of harmony lulls him in his bowers."
3. "None will flatter the poor."
4. "My clansmen's blood demands revenge."
5. "I thank thee, Roderick, for the word."

MODEL. The dishes of luxury *covered* his table *yesterday*.

1. We have seen that there is but one change in any verb to represent differences in time, and that is to relate a *past* act or event.

2. You now see that as we have three different sorts or periods of time—*Past, Present,* and *Future*—we must use an Auxiliary Verb to denote any time *except the Present and the Past.*

If I say "Anna studies Geography," you cannot tell the exact time. But can you tell *in which of the three principal periods* of time she does it?

If I say Anna studied Arithmetic, can you tell *when?*

If I say Anna will study Grammar, can you tell *when?*

LESSON XXV.

Compound Tenses.

1. When we wish to make very nice distinctions of time we divide each Tense into two forms, using the *Past Participle* of the Verb, the little Verb *has* or *have* being placed before it. Thus,

"John *has studied*," denotes an action done *previous* to the time of stating it, but in a period which includes the *present*. This we call the *Prior Present Tense,* which means *previous to* and *in the present.**

2. "John *had studied*" denotes the same act at a past time, and previous to some other past time. This we call the *Prior Past Tense.*

3. "John *will have studied*" denotes the same act at a past time as reckoned from some future time. This we call the *Prior Future Tense.*

This gives us three Tenses and two forms of each

$$\begin{cases} \textit{Present Tense,} \\ \textit{Prior Present Tense,} \\ \textit{Past Tense,} \\ \textit{Prior Past Tense,} \\ \textit{Future Tense,} \\ \textit{Prior Future Tense.} \end{cases}$$

PRACTICE.

1. Each pupil write a short story, telling something he has noticed since the recitation commenced.

2. Each pupil write a story, telling what has occurred within this day, or this week, or this term, or this year.

---

* Used alone, "has" is a Verb, Present Tense, "studied" is a Past Participle. Placed thus together in Predicate, the two Tenses combine, forming the Past Present—or better, Prior Present Tense.

CAUTION 1. In the use of Verbs, select the one that means just what you wish to say.

It is not correct to say " Let us *set* down and rest."
> Say, sit down.

It is not correct to say " John rose up his head."
> Say, raised up his head.

It is not correct to say "John, you may *lay* down."
> Say, you may lie down.

It is not correct to say "Can you *learn* me to read German ? "
> Say, can you teach me to read German ?

2. Never use a Verb immediately after the Verbs *have, has,* or *had*. But the use of a Participle is proper.

It is not correct to say " I would not have *went*." Use the Participle, and say, I would not have *gone*.

> *Wrong.* Dennis has *shook* the carpet.
> *Right.* Dennis has *shaken* the carpet.
> *Wrong.* I *have began* to study Grammar.
> *Right.* I *have begun* to study Grammar.
> *Wrong.* George, you *hadn't ought* to do that.
> *Right.* George, you ought not to do that.

3. Do not attempt to use a Participle alone as Predicate, for *one* word in Predicate must be a *verb*.

> *Wrong.* Who *done* that ?
> *Right.* Who *did* that ?
> *Wrong.* I *seen* him when he *done* it.
> *Right.* I *saw* him when he *did* it.

CRITICISM 1. Did the Frenchman use our language correctly when, having fallen into the water, he said, "I *will* drown, because no one *shall* help me out ? " How should he have expressed his fears ?

2. Did the boy use good English who said, " I have learned all my lesson yesterday ? "

Correct the following ERRORS :

3. John, *shall* you please assist me to learn my lesson ?

4. I *saw* not Jane to-day. Have you saw her ?

5. So far I recited my lesson perfectly every day this week.

6. Lucy *recites* well every day this week.

LESSON XXVI.

Participles—Two Sorts.

1. *Participles* are so much like Verbs that we place them here.

They are *partly* Verbs and *partly* something else. They are changed in form and office, but have the same *meaning* as their Verbs. Thus,

Verbs.	Participles.		Verbs.	Participles.	
Love,	loving,	loved.	Sit,	sitting,	sat.
See,	seeing,	seen.	Know,	knowing,	known.
Feel,	feeling,	felt.	Sing,	singing,	sung.
Go,	going,	gone.	work,	working,	worked.

2. *From each Verb are formed two Participles—the First and the Second—called also the Present and the Past.*

Loving, loved.   Seeing, seen.

The First or Present Participle is formed by adding the letters "ing" to the Verb.

Work + ing, working.   Play + ing, playing.

The Second or Past Participle of Regular Verbs is formed by adding "d" or "ed" to the Verb.

Work + ed, worked.   Play + ed, played.

In the Regular Verbs the Past Tense of the Verb and the Past Participle are alike in form.

VERB	*Present.* Love,	recite,	instruct,
	Past. Loved,	recited,	instructed.
PARTICIPLE	*Present.* Loving,	reciting,	instructing,
	Past. Loved,	recited,	instructed.

The Second Participles of Irregular Verbs are formed variously. Thus,

Verb. Irregular.	Participle. Present.	Past.	Verb. Irregular.	Participle. Present.	Past.
Go,	going,	gone.	Think,	thinking,	thought.
See,	seeing,	seen.	Do,	doing,	done.
Sit,	sitting,	sat.	Lie,	lying,	lain.
Set,	setting,	set.	Write,	writing,	written.

Every Participle has the same meaning as its Verb, but cannot alone make a complete statement. When used in Predicate it must have some Verb in the same Predicate.

How Used.

Remember—A Participle may be used—

1. As a Name—*Singing* is a pleasant exercise.
2. As an Adjective—*Singing* birds delight us.
3. As an Adverb—'Tis *passing* strange.
4. In Predicate with a Verb—Time is *passing* away.
5. As Leader of a Phrase—*Passing* through the grove.

PRACTICE.

1. Each pupil make a Sentence using the Participle *studying* as a Noun.

2. Each pupil make a Sentence using the Participle *running* as an Adjective.

3. Each pupil make a Sentence using the Participle *reciting* in Predicate with " was."

4. In the following Sentences fill the blanks with Participles.

    (a) The sails are all ——.
    (b) The morning sun is ——.
    (c) The pleasant spring is ——.
    (d) The scattered flocks are ——.
    (e) The anchor is ——.
    (f) The gentle winds are ——.

LESSON XXVII.

Irregular Verbs.

Because most Verbs add *d* or *ed* to form their Past Tense and Past Participle, they are called *Regular Verbs*.

But those Verbs that form their Past Tense and Past Participle differently and irregularly are called *Irregular Verbs*.

The Irregular Verbs most frequently used are the following : *

1. These have their Present Tense, Past Tense, and Past Participle alike.

Present.	Past.	Past Part.	Present.	Past.	Past Part.
Beat,	beat,	beat, beaten.	Rid,	rid,	rid.
Burst,	burst,	burst.	Set,	set,	set.
Bet,	bet,	bet.	Shed,	shed,	shed.
Cast,	cast,	cast.	Shut,	shut,	shut.
Cost,	cost,	cost.	Spit,	spit.	spit.
Cut,	cut,	cut.	Split,	split,	split.
Hit,	hit,	hit.	Spread,	spread,	spread.
Hurt,	hurt,	hurt.	Sweat,	sweat,	sweat.
Let,	let,	let.	Thrust,	thrust,	thrust.
Put,	put,	put.	Wet,	wet,	wet.

These have their Past Tense and Past Participle alike, but not like the Present.

Present.	Past.	Past Part.	Present.	Past.	Past Part.
Bend,	bent,	bent.	Lose,	lost,	lost.
Bind,	bound,	bound.	Make,	made,	made.
Bleed,	bled,	bled.	Mean,	meant,	meant.
Bring,	brought,	brought.	Meet,	met,	met.

---

* For a full list see the Normal Grammar.

This list contains the most important Verbs in our language, because most frequently used—and the Past Tense and the Past Participle are so frequently misused that they should be committed to memory

Present.	Past.	Past Part.	Present.	Past.	Past Part.
Buy,	bought,	bought.	Read,	read,	read.
Catch,	caught,	caught.	Ride,	rode,	rode.
Creep,	crept,	crept.	Say,	said,	said.
Feed,	fed,	fed.	Sell,	sold,	sold.
Feel,	felt,	felt.	Send,	sent,	sent.
Fight,	fought,	fought.	Sing,	sung, sang,	sung.
Find,	found,	found.	Sit,	sat,	sat.
Fling,	flung,	flung.	Spring,	sprung, sprang,	sprung.
Have,	had,	had.	Stand,	stood,	stood.
Hear,	heard,	heard.	Strike,	struck,	struck.
Hold,	held,	held.	Sweep,	swept,	swept.
Keep,	kept,	kept.	Teach,	taught,	taught.
Lay,	laid,	laid.	Tell,	told,	told.
Lead,	led,	led.	Think,	thought,	thought.
Leave,	left,	left.	Weep,	wept,	wept.
Lend,	lent,	lent.			

These have different forms for the Present, the Past, and the Past Participle.

Present.	Past.	Past Part.	Present.	Past.	Past Part.
Be, } Am, }	was,	been.	Give,	gave,	given.
			Go,	went,	gone.
Arise,	arose,	arisen.	Grow,	grew,	grown.
Begin,	began,	begun.	Hide,	hid,	hidden.
Bite,	bit,	bitten.	Know,	knew,	known.
Blow,	blew,	blown.	Lie,	lay,	lain.
Choose,	chose,	chosen.	Rise,	rose,	risen.
Come,	came,	come.	Run,	ran,	run.
Do,	did,	done.	See,	saw,	seen.
Draw,	drew,	drawn.	Shake,	shook,	shaken.
Drink,	drank,	drunk.	Slay,	slew,	slain.
Drive,	drove,	driven.	Slide,	slid,	slidden.
Eat,	ate or eat,	eaten.	Steal,	stole,	stolen.
Fall,	fell,	fallen.	Swim,	swam,	swum.
Fly,	flew,	flown.	Take,	took,	taken.
Forget,	forgot,	forgotten.	Wear,	wore,	worn.
Forsake,	forsook,	forsaken.	Write,	wrote,	written.
Freeze,	froze,	frozen.			

LESSON XXVIII.

Be, Am, Is, Are, Was, Were.

The most irregular, most common, and most important Verb in our language is the little Verb *be*. It puts on, in its various conditions, these six distinct forms, *be, am, is, are, was,* and *were*.

Used alone, or as a Principal Verb, it is called a *Neuter Verb*, because it then neither asserts action given nor received, but simple *existence*. Thus,

Lucy *is*. Horses *are*.

Used as an auxiliary with some other word in Predicate, it is called a *Copulative Verb*, because it couples together the other part of a Predicate to its Subject. Thus,

Laughing Lucy.	Lucy laughing.
Singing Anna.	Anna singing.
Running horses.	Horses running.
Wounded bird.	Bird wounded.
Cheerful Mary.	Mary cheerful.

These words, "laughing," "singing," "running," "wounded," and "cheerful," used only with the Nouns, are merely Adjectives—descriptive words. They do not alone make Predicates.

But by placing one of the *Copulative Verbs* between one of them and its Noun, we *declare* the quality denoted by the Adjective, or the act indicated by the Participle. Thus,

Lucy *is* laughing.
Anna *is* singing.
Horses *are* running.
The bird *was* wounded.
Mary *is* cheerful.

So we see that the little familiar words, *is, was, are, were,* serve chiefly to make *Predicates* of Adjectives, Participles, and Nouns.

Words that make a complete Predicate, without the use of Adjectives, Participles, or Nouns, are called *complete* Verbs. Other Verbs are *helping* Verbs.

1. Boys *study*.

This is a complete Sentence; because the Verb "study" makes a full statement concerning "boys."

2. Boys *studying*.

This is not a Sentence; for no complete statement is made.

3. Boys *are*.

This is a complete Sentence—asserting only the *existence of* "boys."

4. Boys *are studying*.

This is also a complete Sentence; but it makes quite a different statement from the last. The Verb "are" makes the statement, while the Participle "studying" shows what the statement is—the character of the action.

5. Boys *are studious*.

This is a complete Sentence; "are" makes the statement, and the Adjective "studious" shows what the statement is.

6. Boys *are students*.

This is a complete Sentence; the Noun "students" shows what is predicated of "boys."

The most frequent and most important use of this Verb, in its various forms, is to put the *actions, conditions, qualities,* and *classes* of subjects *into Predications.*

When we use this Verb in Predicate, its form is determined by the Person and Number of its Subject and by the Tense. Thus,

Present Tense.		*Past Tense.*	
I am,	We ⎫	I ⎱ was,	We ⎫
Thou art,	You ⎬ are.	He ⎰	You ⎬ were.
He is,	They ⎭	Thou wast,	They ⎭

In the Prior (compound) Tenses the second Participle *been* is used with the Auxiliary Verbs *has, have,* and *had* as in corresponding Tenses of other Verbs. Thus,

John *has been* learning his lesson.	They *had been absent* a month.
We *have seen* the elephant.	We *shall be* at home to morrow.

LESSON XXIX.

Sentences with Objects.

NOUNS.

Any Noun may be the *object* of a Sentence.

PRONOUNS.

The following Pronouns may be the Object of Sentences:

Me, thee, him, her, it, us, you, them, whom, that, what, which; also all Pronouns derived from Adjectives.

"We rather visit the *wise* and the *learned* than the *rich* and the *proud.*"

Any word that may be the object of a Sentence may also be the Object of a *Phrase.*

PRACTICE.

1. Let each pupil make a Sentence having the word *house* as the Object.

2. Let each pupil make a Sentence telling what *places* you have visited.

3. Let each pupil make a Sentence telling what *books* you have read.

4. Let each pupil make a Sentence telling what *animals* you like best.

5. Each pupil make a Sentence for each of the Pronouns given above as Objects.

6. Make a Sentence using the words *him, her, it,* and *them.*

Let "him" stand for Ernest, "her" for Anna, "it" for the rabbit, "them" for ducks and chickens.

CRITICISM. Is it correct to say, "I did not learn who Balkam married."

Was it correct to say, "Robert promised you and I a ride on the lake."

Did Charles use good English when he asked, "Did you see Cora and I in the boat?"

Did you notice Ralph and she at the lecture?

Why is it not correct to say "Who did you see there?"

Passive Subjects.

If Columbus *discovered* America, it is as true that America *was discovered* by Columbus.

If Donald *saw* the comet, it is equally true that the comet *was seen* by Donald.

We see now that the same fact can often be stated in two ways :

1. We may make the name of the actor the Subject.

"Brutus killed Cæsar."

Here Brutus performed the act expressed by the Verb "killed," and the word "Brutus" is the Subject of the Sentence.

When the actor or agent is the Subject, the Predicate may be a *Verb*, which denotes the act, or it may be the *Present Participle* of that Verb joined to the *Copulative Verb.*

"Brutus was killing Cæsar."

These are called the *Active forms*—sometimes called "Active voice."

2. We may use the name of the person or thing that *receives* the action expressed by the Predicate as Subject.

"Cæsar was killed by Brutus."

Here "Cæsar," who received—suffered the action, is made the Subject, and the Predicate is the Past Participle of the Verb, joined to the Copulative Verb in one of its forms.*

---

* Pupils should learn to distinguish between a *Verb* and a *Predicate*. A *Verb* is *one word*. It may alone form a Predicate, or it may assist another Verb, an Adjective, a Participle, or a Noun to form a Predicate.

But a *Predicate* is such a word or words as declare something of its Subject. It may be an act done *by* its Subject, or done *to* it. It may be a *quality*, a *state*, or a *thing* declared of its Subject. While every Predicate must have a Verb, either used alone or as its first word, the important word may be a Participle, an Adjective, or a Noun, and the Verb only copulative. Hence, when we speak of "Passive Voice," we speak of the *Subject* as "passive," not the *Verb*;—for English Verbs have no "Passive Voice."

LESSON XXX.

Adjectives.

That old man found a rude boy upon his tree stealing apples.

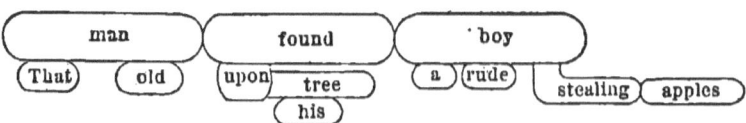

Which old man ?
What kind of man ?
What kind of boy?
Upon *whose* trees ?
Doing what ?

For what purpose did you use the word "that?"
For what did you use the word "old?"
For what did you use the word "his?"
For what did you use the word "stealing?"

Remember— Words that describe things—telling what, whose, how many, or what kind of things, are called Adjectives.

What?.......*This* boy, *that* boy, *the* boy, *yonder* boy.
Whose?......*My* friend, *our* friend, *your* friend, *their* friend.
How many?.. *One* friend, *ten* friends, *all* men, *some* boys.
What sort?...*Red* apple, *green* apple, *sweet* apple, *winter* apple.

PRACTICE.

I.

Select all the Adjectives in the following Sentences :

"When early morning's ruddy light
  Bids man to labor go,
We haste with scythes all sharp and bright
  The meadow's grass to mow."

" Ripe, red apples—oh, how nice !
Buttered bread—a precious slice!
I ittle Nelly, good and fair,
Will her joy with Johnny share."

II.

In the following Sentences fill the blanks with appropriate Adjectives.

1. " Mary had —— —— lamb ; —— fleece was —— as snow."
2. There in —— —— mansion —— to rule,
—— —— master taught —— —— school.

III.

Make a Sentence using the word " good."

Make a Sentence using the two words " large " and " sweet."

Make a Sentence using the three words " our," " new," " white."

Make a Sentence using the three Adjectives, '' my," " beautiful," " green."

Remember—Adjectives are attached to Nouns. For as in language a person or a thing must be represented by a Noun, so the *quality, sort,* or *condition* of the person or thing must be denoted by the Adjective.

Classes of Adjectives.

We have three different sorts of Adjectives.

1. Those which point out an individual *thing* from a *class* of things.

This book, *that* book, *my* book, *one* book, *ten* books—such are called *Specifying Adjectives.*

2. Those which denote a quality of a person or thing.

Good apple, *red* apple, *sweet* apple, *wise* man—such are called *Qualifying Adjectives.*

3. Those which denote some act or condition.

Running brook, *opening* flower, *baked* apple — such are called *Verbal Adjectives.*

LESSON XXXI.

Qualifying Adjectives.

What is the *color* of a lemon ?
What is the *shape* of an orange ?

Thus, "Yellow" is one of the qualities of a lemon.
"Round" expresses one of the qualities of an orange.

DEFINITION. *Those words that denote some quality of a person or thing is a Qualifying Adjective.*

1. *Amiable*..She is an amiable young lady.
2. *Meek* .....She is almost as *meek* as Moses.
3. *Ripe*.....*Ripe* apples are rare in June.
4. *Tall*......Tall oaks from little acorns grow.

Specifying Adjectives.

Is *this* hat yours ?   Have you seen *my* book ?
Will you have *ten* oranges or *twelve?*

DEFINITION. *Those Adjectives that distinguish individual things from others of the same sort are Specifying Adjectives.*

This........This book is mine.
That........That book is yours.
My ....My book is lost.
Their ....Their throat is an open sepulchre.
One........One lesson well learned is better.

SUB-CLASSES.

Specifying Adjectives include three sub-classes, called *Pure Adjectives, Possessive Adjectives, Numeral Adjectives.*

Pure.

Specifying Adjectives that answer the question which, are called Pure Specifiers.

Which book? *This* book. *Which* boy? *That* boy.

Numeral.

Adjectives that denote a number are called Numeral Adjectives. These answer the question *how many?*

" *Some* men said *one* thing and some another."

" The *sixth* angel sounded."

Possessive.

Adjectives that denote possession or that have possessive forms are called Possessive Adjectives. They answer the question *whose?*

Children's shoes, *men's* boots, *my* cap, *our* father.

" Beauty's tears are lovelier than *her* smile."

Verbal Adjectives.

We *laugh* with *laughing* children.

We *weep* with *weeping* children.

DEFINITION. *All Adjectives derived from Verbs are Verbal Adjectives.*

1. " *Running* streams afford pure water."

" Running " describes " streams ; " it is therefore an Adjective.

2. That boy *running* across the fields is a truant.

" Running " describes " boy ; " it is therefore an Adjective.

DEFINITION. *Adjectives derived from Proper Names are called Proper Adjectives.*

England—*English* customs. Newton—*Newtonian* theory.

LESSON XXXII.

Adjectives.

COMPARING.

1. The river is *deep*.
2. The lake is *deeper*.

Both Sentences declare the same property. But one declares a *greater amount* of the quality.

> Our Concord grapes are sweet.
> Our Delawares   are sweet*er*.
> Our Crevillings   are sweet*est*.

2. These statements show that the same quality may exist in different degrees ; and that most Qualifying Adjectives have *changes of form* to show the comparisons.

The common form of the Adjective is called the *Positive form*. We add *er* to the Positive to make the *Comparative form,* and *est* * for the *Superlative*.

Remember (1.)—When we compare *two* things by means of Adjectives we use the *comparative* form.

The Delaware grape is sweet*er* than the Concord.

Here the Delaware grape is compared with the Concord by the *er* added to sweet.

---

* When the Adjective is a long word we do not make it longer by adding *er* or *est* to it; but we place the word *more* or *most* before the Adjective. Thus, *more* amiable, *more* considerate. It is not correct to say "the rose is the beautiful*est* flower in the garden ; but the rose is the *most beautiful* flower in the garden. Nor do we say the rose is beautiful*er* than the dandelion, but "the rose is *more* beautiful than the dandelion."

(2.) When we compare *more than two,* we use the Superlative form.

> The Crevelling is the sweet*est* of the three.
> John is the largest * boy in school.

It is not correct to say, "One is the tallest of the two."

Did Sarah speak correctly when she said, "Eve was the fairest of all her daughters"?

Adjectives that denote qualities that cannot be varied in amount, cannot be compared. Thus,

If a thing is *perfect* we cannot add to the quality—so the Adjective "perfect" cannot be compared.

PRACTICE.

Read the following riddle and point out all the Adjectives in it.

"I know a curious and wonderful house, in which are two small windows. At this window a painter ever sits, who paints all things that he sees through them—black, white, red, green, and blue, long, short, round, pointed and cornered in the most perfect manner.

"There is nothing so large or so wonderful in this great earth of ours that he cannot make a faithful picture of, and that on a surface as tiny as a common bean. Also he paints every thought and fancy of the master of the house, so that they who pass by, glancing up at the little windows, may readily discern them. If the master is glad, the windows look bright and glistening; but if he is sad, a pearly mist clouds them.

"And when the master is weary and would rest, then Mors puts up the shutters, to shade the light from him, and folk walk softly past the house saying mournfully, 'The little windows are broken.'"

Separate those Adjectives into the three classes — the *Qualifying,* the *Specifying,* the *Verbal.*

Now, if you can, you may guess the riddle.

---

* In adding *er* or *est* to Adjectives that end in *e* or *y,* observe the rule for spelling which you find in your spelling-book.

LESSON XXXIII.

Adjectives in Predicate.

That large red apple is sweet.

Which word *points out* the apple you talk about?
Which word tells the *color* of apple?
Which word tells the *size?*
Which word tells the *taste?*
How many Adjectives in that Sentence?

If we take away all the Adjectives and write the other words we shall have the two words,

Apple is.

Although these two words form a Sentence, they do not express the thought we wish to convey, for we naturally ask *apple is what?* and the ready answer is,

Apple is sweet.

Thus we see that some Adjectives are *used with a Verb,* to help *declare* something of the Subject.

Remember—An Adjective is used in Predicate when the Verb requires its aid to make the statement.

That large sweet apple *is red.*

Now which Adjective helps *declare* something of apple?

That sweet red apple *is large.*

Now which Adjective is in Predicate?

*Remember—An Adjective in Predicate generally describes the Subject—*sometimes the *Object.*

The Subject..1. William *appears sad.*
2. Ernest *was happy* then.
3. Charles *has become rich.*
The Object...4. Benevolence *makes man happy.*

CAUTION. Do not give the Adverbial form to Adjectives in Predicate

> *Wrong.*   1. John *feels badly* to-night.
>
>   2. Can any one *feel gladly?*
>
> *Corrected.* 1. John *feels bad* to-night.
>
>   2. Can any one *feel glad?*

PRACTICE.

I.

In the following Sentences fill the blanks with suitable Adjectives in Predicate.

Grass is ——. John has been —— that he lost his kite.

Sugar is ——. William will be —— to find his knife.

The earth is ——. We all should be —— of his good fortune.

No man can be —— unless he is——

II.

Make Sentences declaring two qualities of water.

Make Sentences declaring three properties of glass.

Make Sentences declaring four properties of gold.

Make Sentences declaring three similar properties of the sun, the earth, and the moon.

MODEL. Glass is *solid, transparent,* and *brittle.*

III.

Make Sentences comparing *two* rivers *as to length.*

Make Sentences comparing two lakes as to *size.*

Make Sentences comparing three mountains as to *height.*

Make Sentences comparing two birds as to *size.*

Make Sentences comparing two animals as to *beauty.*

Make Sentences comparing two cities as to *latitude.*

MODEL. Chicago is *farther north* than St. Louis.

LESSON XXXIV.

Nouns and Pronouns in Predicate.

Peter was an apostle.

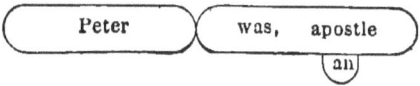

What is the Subject of this Sentence?

What is said of Peter?

Do the words "Peter" and "apostle" refer to the same man?

Ans.—"Peter" is the name of the *man.* "Apostle" is the name of his *office.*

Thus the whole Predicate, "was an apostle," declares the office of "Peter."

Remember—Nouns, like Adjectives and Participles, may be in Predicate with Copulative Verbs to declare some title, office, or attribute of the Subject.

1. Thou *art a scholar.*   2. We *are friends.*
3. Washington was commander of the American army.
4. Sherman is General-in-chief of the Army.
5. Burr was a disgrace to the American name.
6. New York is the richest State in the Union.

PRACTICE.

Make a Sentence declaring an office of St. Paul.

Make a Sentence declaring an attribute of Geo. Peabody.

Make a Sentence declaring an office of Victoria.

Make a Sentence declaring an attribute of Benedict Arnold.

Make a Sentence declaring an attribute of the moon.

Make a Sentence declaring the occupation of yourself.

Remember—By suppressing the Copulative Verb, these offices, attributes, and titles of persons and things may be *assumed* without being declared. Thus,

Peter the Apostle.

" Peter the Hermit resembled, in character, Peter the *Apostle.*"

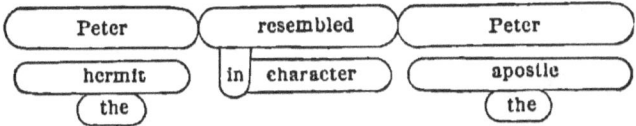

What is the Subject of this Sentence ?—"Peter."

What is the Object ?—" Peter."

Then " Peter resembled Peter."

What words distinguish the Subject from the Object?

But " Hermit " is a *name* of a condition of life, and

Apostle is the *name* of an office or occupation.

DEFINITION. *" One Noun used to explain some office or attribute of another Noun going before, is in Apposition."*

Such words perform offices similar to those of Adjectives —but not exactly like Adjectives. They are Nouns in fact —Adjectives by inference, because they show which person of a class is meant.

Webster the *statesman* was Secretary of State.

Webster the *lexicographer* wrote the Unabridged Dictionary.

PRACTICE.

1. Write a Sentence in which Columbus shall be described by a Noun in Apposition.

2. Write a Sentence in which Washington shall be described by two Nouns in Apposition.

3. Describe Lincoln by the use of three Nouns in Apposition.

4. Describe Niagara Falls by a Noun in Apposition.

5. Write about the second President of the United States—distinguish him from his son by a Noun in Apposition.

6. Distinguish two men named Douglass by Nouns in Apposition.

LESSON XXXV.

Adverbs.

ILLIAM works.

2. William *often* works.

3. William *seldom* works.

4. William *never* works.

These four Sentences show the influence of Adverbs to modify or change the meaning of the Predicate.

Each Sentence has the same Subject and Predicate, yet they all differ in their meanings, because of the Adverbs "*often*," "*seldom*," "*never*."

What is an Adverb?

DEFINITION. *An Adverb is any word that modifies or changes the meaning of a Verb, of an Adjective, or of another Adverb.*

Of a Verb.....1. William works *often*.
            2. William works *well*.
            3. *There* comes the train.
Of Adjectives..4. Is it *very easy* to mow ?
            5. William is *exceedingly* diligent.
Of Adverbs....6. The cars move *very* rapidly.

"Often" tells *when*, "well" tells *how*, "there" tells *where*.

Classes.

Remember—Some Adverbs tell *how* a thing is done, some tell *where*, some tell *when*, some *why*. Those that answer the question—

How ?   are Adverbs of *manner*.."Speak *gently* to the
                             little child."

Where ? are Adverbs of *place*..... "*Here* sleeps he now alone."

When ? are Adverbs of *time*...... "I shall go *soon*."

Why ? are Adverbs of *cause*..... "*Therefore* am I come."

PRACTICE.

In the following Sentences point out the Adverbs and tell the sort.

1. " Vainly we offer each ample oblation."
2. " Brilliantly the glassy waters mirror back his smiles."
3. " The very rich man can never be truly happy."
4. " I have always been an admirer of happy human faces."

Fill the blanks with appropriate Adverbs.

1. John recites —— to-day.
2. The wind blew —— and the rain fell ——.
3. I think we shall —— have a better time to learn than we have ——.
4. Does William recite —— than George ?

Make Sentences, using one of the following Adverbs in each.

Now.	Here.	Soon.	Not.	Brilliantly.
Then.	There.	Thus.	Never.	Vainly.
Often.	Yonder.	Clearly.	Nowhere.	Cheerfully.
Seldom.	Hither.	Well.	Negatively.	Dolefully.

COMPARISON.

Anna will come soon.

Clara will come soon*er*.

Mary will come soon*est*.

The above statements show that the same Adverb may express differences in its modification. So that some

Adverbs may be compared like Adjectives.

LESSON XXXVI.

Prepositions.

AUL stands *on the bridge.*

Stands *where?*

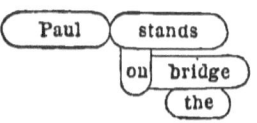

Here you see the little word "on" links the word "bridge" to the word "stands."

And the three words, "on the bridge," thus put together, tell *where* "Paul stands."

Ernest walks *through the brook.*

Walks *where?*

The dog stands........*where?*

Stands *in the water.*

1. In our language we have very many of these *groups of words* that, together, answer such questions as *When? Where? How?* Most of these groups begin with the little words *at, by, for, in, of, on, to, under, with,* and many others that are *placed before* Nouns and Pronouns and connect them to other words.

These little words are called *Prepositions.*

1. We arrived *at* Albany *at* noon.
2. We passed *by* Utica.

3. We went *from* home *in* the morning.

4. We returned *on* the last day *of* vacation.

5. We went *to* the recitation *with* our teacher.

What is a *Preposition?*

2. DEFINITION. *A Preposition is a word used to connect other words by showing some relation between them.*

1. The wisdom *of* Solomon.

"*Of* ' shows a relation of *possession.*

"Of Solomon" answers the question *whose* "wisdom."

2. They passed *under* the cloud.

"*Under*" shows a relation of *place.*

"Under the cloud" answers the question "passed *where?*"

3. Ralph has been absent *since* Saturday.

"Since" shows a relation of *time.*

"Since Saturday" answers the question "*how long?*"

4. We returned *in* the evening.

"In" shows a relation of *time.*

"In the evening" answers the question "*when?*"

In example (1) would "of" alone tell *whose* wisdom?

In example (2) would "under" alone tell *where* they passed?

Would "since" alone tell *how long* Ralph has been absent?

Phrases.

3. Then we see it often requires *two or more words* put together to answer some questions, or to perform certain offices in Sentences.

Such groups of words are called *Phrases.*

LESSON XXXVII.

Let us see if we can understand what a Phrase is.

1. *A Phrase is a structure, built of words, as a Sentence is. Yet it is not a Sentence;* for it has no *Subject* and no *Predicate.* It does not make a complete Statement.

A Phrase is used to help make a Sentence, just as we use Nouns, and Adjectives, and Adverbs. Thus, if I say " *Virtue* makes man happy," and " *To be good* makes man happy," I make two separate Sentences which mean about the same thing. The Subject of the first is a *Noun* ("virtue"). That of the second is a *Phrase* ("to be good"). So that the three words put together fill the place of Subject; just as a Noun does.

American history is an interesting study.

What history?

The history *of America* is an interesting study.

Here we see the word "*American*" tells *what* history, and the two words "*of America*" tell the same thing. Hence, if "American" is an Adjective, so is the Phrase "of America." Once more—

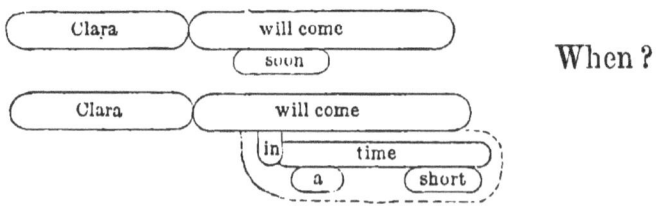

When ?

Here the four words "in a short time" make a Phrase that means just what we mean by the word "soon." But "soon" is a *word Adverb*, and "in a short time" is a *Phrase Adverb.*

Now you understand what we mean by a *Phrase.*

2. Definition. *A Phrase is two or more words so combined as to perform the office of a Noun, of an Adjective, or of an Adverb.*

3. Definition. *A Phrase beginning with a Preposition is called a Prepositional Phrase.*

In Diagram we place the Preposition first, linking the Noun or Pronoun following to the word that the Phrase modifies. Thus,

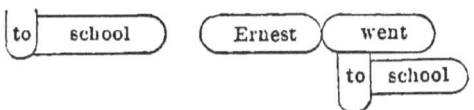

"To" links "school" to "went."

4. *But some Phrases begin with another sort of words called Participles.*

What is a Participle?

5. *A Participle is a word that partakes of both a Verb and an Adjective*—sometimes a *Verb* and a *Noun*.

6. *All Participles are derived from Verbs,* retaining the meaning of their verbs; but they do not alone make a statement. [See p. 61.]

Verb.	*Participle.*	
See,	seeing......1.	Jane, *seeing the elephant*, fainted.
Hear,	hearing.....2.	John, *hearing the bell*, went to school.
Find,	finding.....3.	*Finding fault* never does any good.

7. *Remember—A Phrase beginning with a Participle is called a Participial Phrase.*

Thus, in the Sentences above—

"Seeing the elephant," "hearing the bell," and "finding fault" are *Participial Phrases*.

LESSON XXXVIII.

Offices of Phrases.

When we use Phrases in making Sentences we give them their *official names*. Thus,

1. *A Phrase used as we use a Noun is a Noun Phrase.* It is also called a *Substantive Phrase.*

Finding fault never does any good.
> *What* never does any good ?

To do good is the duty of all.
> *What* is the duty of all ?

You see the Phrase " finding fault " is the subject of one Sentence, and " to do good " is the Subject of the other, thus filling the office of Nouns.

2. A *Noun Phrase* (Substantive Phrase) may also be the *Object* of a Sentence.

I doubted *his having been a soldier.*
> I doubted—what ? *

3. *Remember—A Phrase used as Adjunct to a Noun is an Adjective Phrase.*

1. " The time *of the singing of birds has come.*"
> What time ?

Of the singing of birds.

" Of the singing of birds " tells *what* time has come, and is an Adjective Phrase.

" Of birds " tells *whose* singing—(*bird's* singing)—it is therefore an Adjective Phrase.

---

* Not " his "—nor " having "—nor " been "—nor " a "—nor " soldier." But *put those words together* and they tell just *what* I doubted. So a wagon-maker puts together a *hub*, felloes and spokes, to make what ? a wagon ?—no ; but a *wheel.* Yet a wheel is a part of a wagon.

Change the following Word Adjectives to equivalent Phrase Adjectives :

1. The *eastern* star fades at the day's coming.
2. The *morning* mists are rolling away.
3. The *summer* days are coming.
4. Have you read *St. Paul's* epistle to the Romans ?

Change the following Phrase Adjectives to equivalent Word Adjectives :

5. " The mists of the morning are rolling away."
6. " The foam *of the billows* already I see."
7. The heart *of me* is entranced into the high realm *of beauty.*
8. " A thing *of beauty* is a joy forever."

Adverbial.

4. *Remember*—A Phrase used as we use an Adverb is an *Adverbial Phrase.*

1. The boat went *over the falls* ...... Adverb of *place.*
   Went .... *where ?*

2. It was not found *until Monday* .... Adverb of *time.*
   Found .... *when ?*

3. *For this purpose* have I raised } .. Adverb of *cause.*
   thee up.
   Raised .... *wherefore ?*

4. We can learn this lesson only } .. Adverb of *manner.*
   by hard study.
   Learn .... *how ?*

LESSON XXXIX.

Sentences Made to Order.

1. Each pupil make a Sentence adapted to this Diagram.

1.

MODEL. Birds sing.

2. Each pupil make a Sentence for this Diagram.

2.

MODEL. Some birds sing sweetly.

3. Each pupil make a Sentence for this Diagram.

3.

MODEL. Most birds sing in the morning.

4. Each pupil write a Sentence for this Diagram.

4.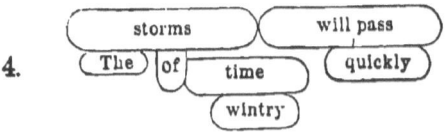

MODEL. Have the pupils of this class recited well?

5. Each pupil write a Sentence for this Diagram.

5.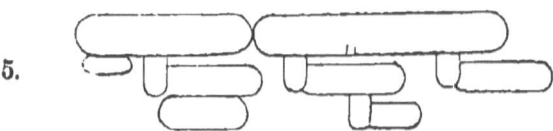

MODEL. At break of day the top of the mountain was covered with clouds.

6. Each pupil write a Sentence for this Diagram.

6.

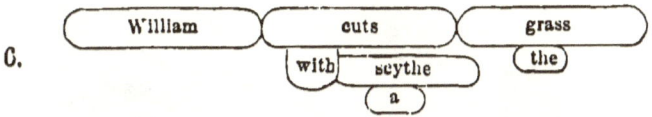

MODEL. Lucy studies her lessons in the evening.

7. Each pupil write a Sentence for this Diagram.

7.

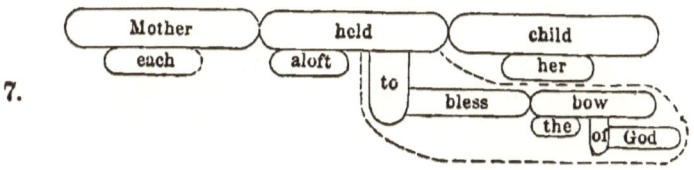

MODEL. The teacher often requests her pupils to write a number of Sentences.

Each pupil complete a Sentence for each of the following Diagrams.

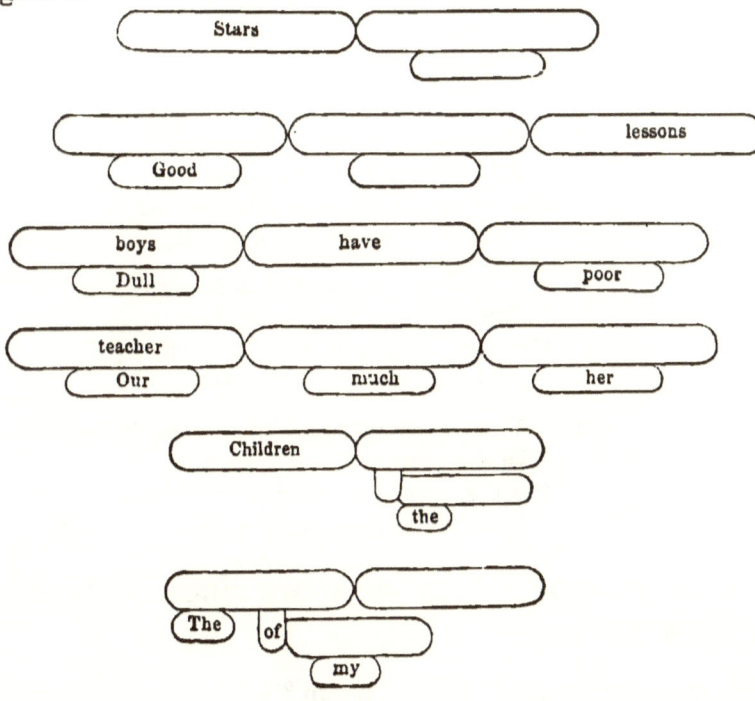

LESSON XL.

1. " In the happy days of boyhood,
 Five-and-thirty years ago,
(Life's golden age of joyhood,)
 We built castles of the snow.

2. " Our castles were the queerest
 Ever reared by human skill ;
And of names we chose the dearest ;—
 That of ours was Bunker Hill.

3. " Boys detailed for service foreign,
 Fell in line with clouded brow ;
Each one clamored to be Warren ;
 And none wanted to be Howe.

4. " Thus we fought the fight of Bunker's,
 In the days that knew no care,
Ere the snow we tossed, as younkers,
 Time had sifted on our hair."

1. A group of four or more lines in poetry is called a *Stanza*.

How many Stanzas in this poem ?

How many Sentences in the first Stanza ?

What is the Subject ?   What is the Predicate ?

Has it an Object ?

Then what sort of Sentence is it ?

When did "we build castles of the snow?"

How many in the second stanza ?—In the third ?

What is the Subject of the *second* Sentence ?

What is the Subject of the third Sentence ?

2. Why is a Comma placed at the end of the first line ?

3. Do you see curved marks ( ) that enclose the third line ?

Marks like those are called *Parentheses*.

Parentheses are used to enclose words *not necessary to form the Sentence*, but simply to add some accidental fact or explanation.

4. In the first word of the third line, notice the little comma between *e* and *s*.

A mark like that is called an *Apostrophe*. It is used *with the s* to show that the word is a *Possessive* Adjective derived from a Noun, [see p. 71.]

NOTICE the *Double Commas* before the first word and also after the last.

NOTICE the mark [;] at the end of the 3th, 7th, 10th, and 11th lines.

A mark like that is called a *Semicolon*.

A Semicolon is used at the end of a Sentence that is followed by another Sentence closely associated with it in thought.

LESSON XLI.

Letter-Writing.

1. One of the most important accomplishments of young people is the art of letter-writing. We should early learn this art. By and by, the boys will be men of business, and most business transactions are by means of letters.

2. Through the medium of letters, boys and girls can pay their absent friends most delightful visits. In writing letters we improve our minds and hearts, and by it we certainly improve our language; for we shall be more careful of our use of words that we put on paper than of those we speak.

3. In letter-writing, it is well to observe the approved forms, and to give to the several parts of a letter their proper positions. These are illustrated in the following MODEL, arranged and written by one of our little pupils.

I.

Rochester, July 4, 1874.

My dear Cousin,

Our school closed yesterday. I was tired; but the noise of the fire-crackers woke me up. I received the prize for spelling; and Papa looked glad when I was called out to take it. It is a nice book. My "recitation" was about "Jack-in-the-Pulpit." Three of us sang "We are happy now, dear Mother;" and happy we all were. We have had a good school; and I expect a pleasant vacation at Grandma's.

Your loving Cousin,

Anna.

1. Every letter should be preceded by
   (1) The DATE, which should include the *place* and the *time*.
   (2) The ADDRESS.
2. Every letter should be closed with
   (1) Some complimentary expression.
   (2) The name of the writer.

In this letter, what is on the first line? On what part of the line?
1. That part of the letter is called the *date*.

What is on the second line? On what part of it?
2. That is the *address*.
3. The next part is the *letter*.

On what part of the line does the letter commence?
Does every distinct Sentence commence with a *capital letter*, and end with a *period?*
4. Directly below the letter is the complimentary title of the writer —called the *close*.

On what part of the line is this written?
5. The last word of every letter should be the *name* of the writer, the *signature*.

On what part of the line is that written?

PRACTICE.

Each pupil write a letter on slate that shall contain three distinct Sentences, and observe the *form* of the MODEL; thus, [Fill the blanks.]

[*Date*] ---

[*Address*] ---

[*Letter*] ---

[*Close*] ---

[*Name*] ---

II.
Each pupil write a letter to an absent *friend*, stating what occurred in school yesterday that you may think of interest to him.

III.
Each pupil write a letter to a *cousin*, stating what studies you have —how you prosper in them—which you like best—what you are to take up next term.

LESSON XLII.

Mystery? *or* Miracle?

It is one of the most wonderful mysteries in the world—almost a miracle—that the thoughts of our minds, and the feelings of our hearts, can find their way down our arms, along our fingers, to the point of a. pen, and there—dissolved in ink—take form and shape on paper. Yet this is done every time we write a letter to a friend.

At first this is a difficult task. But PRACTICE will make it as easy as to talk. Here is a fine Lesson for little ones.

A little brother and sister, who found it difficult to put their thoughts on paper, were induced by their good mother to form "*A Mum Society,*" with these By-Laws to control the meetings:

1. "All words must be written—not one spoken."
2. "All talk on paper must be in complete Sentences."
3. "Every speech shall close with a question."

Below is a report of the proceedings of one meeting:

EDDIE. "Our subject to-day is Rain. Rain is little drops of water. It comes from the clouds. Do you know how the drops get into the clouds?"

CORA. "I do not know how the rain-drops get into the clouds. But mamma says all the clouds are made from the *water* of the ocean and the lakes and rivers. Do you love to be in the rain?"

EDDIE. "In warm weather, I love to stand out in the yard and have the rain fall on my head and arms and hands. But it makes me feel very queer to hold my face up to the rain. Do you know what rain is good for?"

CORA. "Rain is good to water the plants in the garden, so we need not water them with a sprinkler. Rain falls on the roof, and the water runs into the cistern, so we can have good, soft water to wash our faces and to bathe in. Can you tell when it is going to rain?"

EDDIE. "When the thick dark clouds come, I think it will rain; and sometimes I guess right, but not always—so I cannot tell *sure* when it will rain. But they say 'Old Probabilities' can always tell. Who is Old Probabilities?"

CORA. "He is a remarkable man, I suppose, and knows more about the weather than all the world besides. Is it not time to adjourn?"

EDDIE. "This meeting stands adjourned to to-morrow evening. Shall the subject be *Picnics?*"

Do you not think Eddie and Cora will soon learn to talk pretty well on paper? Try this method. You will like it, and become good writers.

PRACTICE.

Let us now put some of our thoughts on paper

1. Each pupil write *three Sentences* that shall express some of the thoughts you had on your way to school.*

2. Each pupil write *five Sentences* on FRUITS, stating—

    1. Where they grow.   2. For what they are used.

    3. State five different kinds you like best.

    4. In what season of the year they are most abundant.

    5. What effect on health.

3. Each pupil write four Sentences on the APPLE, stating—

    1. Where apples grow most abundantly.

    2. Name some of the most common.

    3. Name the sorts you like best.

    4. What four things are made of apples.

4. Put some thoughts on paper about GRAPES.

    1. What are Grapes?   2. On what do they grow?

    3. In what countries do they grow?

    4. In what places do they not grow?   5. Why?

    6. What are some of the best sorts of grapes?

    7. For what are grapes used?

    8. What two things are made of grapes?

    9. What is said about grapes in the Bible?

    10. Each pupil write three Sentences about PEACHES.

    11. Each pupil write three Sentences about MELONS.

    12. Each pupil write three Sentences about SQUASHES.

---

* The teacher should decide (1) how long time may be given to each exercise. (2) Also what system of *examination* and *criticism* shall be adopted, as, (*a*) by personal examination of all the pupils, or, (*b*) by requiring the pupils to exchange slates and criticise one another. By either method let the criticisms include the *spelling*, the *capitals*, the marks of *punctuation*, and the style of *writing*.

LESSON XLIII.

Translations.

Let us translate this *picture* into *words*.

1. EDWARD may tell the class what he sees in the picture.

2. CLASS may mention all the things that Edward has omitted.

3. Each pupil may write a complete Sentence, stating—

What the boys are doing.

EVA may place that Sentence in Diagram on the board.

4 Class write, telling—

What the first boy holds in his hand.

MARY may place the Sentence in Diagram.

What is the *Subject* of the Sentence?

5. Class write, telling—

What the second boy is doing.
What is the *Predicate* of the Sentence ?

6. Class write, telling—

What the third boy is doing.
What is the *Object* of the Sentence?

7. Class write, telling—

What the other boys are doing.
What is the *Subject*, the *Predicate*, and the *Object* of the Sentence ?
RALPH may place the Sentence in Diagram.

8. Class may write *three things* that the girl is doing.

How many Predicates has the Sentence you have now written ?
What word is the Subject of all these Predicates ?

9. You have now written separate Sentences for the different parts of the picture.

For to-morrow's exercise, each member of the class may write on paper a complete story that shall contain all the facts and thoughts that the picture suggests.

Topics.

It is well for every pupil to write at least one composition each day. Below are a few TOPICS adapted to children. The teacher will add others as she may deem proper.

1. KITES.

1. My Kite. 2. My brother's Kite. 3. Franklin's Kite.

[Take *either* or *all* of these and write what you think about them.]

2. PAPERS.

1. Children's Papers. 2. Political Papers, News Papers, Religious Papers.

3. Books.

1. The last Book I read. 2. The Books I like best. 3. The best Book.

4. Pictures.

1. Photographs. 2. Paintings. 3. Engravings. 4. My favorites

5. Toys.

1. Girls' Toys. 2. Boys' Toys. 3. Who else have Toys, and what are they?

6. Leaves.

1. Different sorts. 2. Colors. 3. Forms. 4. Uses of Leaves.

7. Stones.

1. Curb Stones. 2. Paving Stones. 3. Building Stones. 4. Precious Stones.

8. Grain.

1. Different sorts? 2. The uses of each.

9. Flowers.

1. Spring Flowers? 2. Summer Flowers? 3. Autumn Flowers? 4. My favorite Flowers?

10. Work.

1. For Boys? 2. For Girls? 3: For Men? 4. The work I like best?

11. Play.

1. For Boys? 2. For Girls? 3. Our favorite Plays?

12. Games.

1. Summer Games? 2. Winter Games? 3. Home Games?